COURT OF LIES

DYAN CHICK

Illaria Publishing

Cover Artwork by Sanja Balan (Sanja's Covers)
Editing by Elizabeth A. Lance (EAL Editing Services)

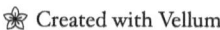 Created with Vellum

Chapter One

"**I**s it true, did you make a deal with a Winter Fae?" The Queen, my mother, looked at me, incredulous. She shook her head. "Those humans taught you no common sense."

The humans denied that magic existed and tried to pretend that the Fae were gone. If not for Nani, I'd know even less than I did now. Now wasn't the time to explain how the human world worked. To be honest, the Queen's lack of understanding made Tristan's favor make more sense. The Fae seemed to have just as little knowledge about humans as the humans did about them.

I glanced at Tristan, then turned away from his sly smirk, focusing back on the Queen. "I needed help, it wasn't a big favor. Tristan, I can answer any of the questions you have about humans right now." Somehow, I knew it wasn't going to be as simple as that. While I continued to go back and forth with Tristan, I had grown to trust him. Maybe I was wrong to do so.

"It's not quite that simple," Tristan said. "I have lots of questions. It could take weeks. I'll need her to stay with me for a while."

"You haven't changed, have you?" Dane said.

I looked at the other three princes, expecting them to say

something to defend me. Shouldn't they ask him to back down? I could tell none of them were happy with the situation, yet none of them seemed ready to pounce.

"She made a verbal commitment to participate in Queen's Trial," Cormac said. "Surely your curiosity can be sated from here?"

Surprised that Cormac hadn't asked for the entire thing to be dropped, I looked back over at Tristan to see his reaction. He was wearing one of his trademark smirks.

"There's no reason she can't be in the Winter Court for a few weeks. I'll return her to you when we're finished and she's repaid her favor."

"Why would I go with you to the Winter Court? Someone tried to kill *you* and somebody captured me and interrogated me. It's not safe there."

"It wasn't safe in the House of the Moon," he corrected.

"You took her to the House of the Moon?" the Queen asked, showing the first sign of motherly concern since I'd arrived. "That isn't exactly a respectable place for a Queen's Trial candidate."

"We'll stay at my palace, you have my word. No trips to the House of the Moon," Tristan said.

"You think it'll be safe there?" I asked. "Your own nobles are moving against you. What makes you think they won't come after you there?"

"It won't be safe for you anywhere, now that you've made your bid for the trial official. It's not a sanctioned part of the trial, but there will be people trying to hurt you. I'm afraid being related to me is going to make things harder on you. You are going to be seen as the biggest threat, especially when they find out about the males who stepped up as your consorts," she said.

"But you said you can't help me; that being your child gives me no benefit," I said.

"That's true. I can't and won't help you. But you've got power you shouldn't have. That makes you a threat."

"Even if I'm not safe anywhere, I already agreed to compete. How can I do that from the Winter Court? It's not even part of the kingdom anymore," I said.

"You don't have to be here for the first several trials, isn't that right, Your Majesty?" Tristan asked.

She frowned, but nodded. "The first few trials are typically done from home. Then, all the girls who successfully complete them get an invitation to the palace to compete at the next level. It looks like the Winter Court might be your home while you complete those first steps."

"You're going to let him take me? Just like that?" I looked at the princes, eyes pleading. "No objections?"

"Favors are serious business here, you have to honor your end," Ethan said, pain etched across his face. "We can't get you out of this."

My stomach twisted into knots. I could tell Ethan was fighting to hold himself back. Whatever I'd gotten into with Tristan was more serious than I imagined. But perhaps, there was a way to make it easier on me. "I'm not going without them," I said turning back to Tristan.

"I'm not having them in my palace," Tristan hesitated, "unless you feel like you can choose between them? I think we'd have room for one."

I glared at Tristan, and clenched my jaw. He knew he was asking me the impossible. I felt the mating bond with Ethan, I knew I had something special with Dane and Cormac. The idea of being apart from any of them made my chest hurt. I'd come this far with them, and I didn't want to continue on without any of them. "You know I can't choose."

"I suppose the three of you could compete to see who could join us?" Tristan suggested. "However, if any of you come, you know how that's going to look. It'll be interesting to see you convince your families that you aren't colluding with the Winter

Court. Especially since you'll be returning with me after spending the last few days there."

My shoulders sank. Tristan was right and he'd put me in an impossible situation. The reputation of the Winter Court wasn't good in Faerie. If any of the princes spent an extended amount of time there it could damage their reputations. I couldn't ask that of them. It wasn't like last time. There weren't any Sodalis attacks to use as an excuse.

Plus, if I didn't have the distractions of any of the other princes, I might be able to fulfill my end of the bargain with Tristan quicker. I knew whatever game he was playing had nothing to do with learning about humans. He had something else up his sleeve, I wasn't sure what it was yet. Whatever his goal, leaving the princes out of it might be the best way to protect them.

"How do you think it's going to look to the other candidates when they find out that the front-runner spent the first several weeks of the trials in an enemy land?" Dane said.

"I suppose it will help her chances even more," Tristan said. "She isn't even Queen yet and she's already working to forge diplomatic ties between Faerie and the Winter Court. There's nothing unusual about sending representatives of the Reagent into another land."

"That's true," the Queen said. "Tiana has typically held the post. Seeing as how she's gone missing, I can't exactly send her as my liaison."

I tensed at the mention of Tiana and hoped it would be a long time before I ever saw her again. Maybe she fell into the Under and the creatures she had befriended turned on her. I had a feeling I wasn't that lucky, but I could hope.

"If it makes you all feel better, I promise to return her here after she passes the first part of the trial. I'll consider the favor paid in full," Tristan said.

"How long is the first part?" I said the words quietly, almost afraid to hear the answer. The fact that no one was objecting immediately, made it feel like it had already been agreed to.

"Three weeks," Ethan said. "Usually. No more than five."

"Five weeks with Tristan? Alone?" I turned to look at Cormac, the usual voice of reason when it came to Tristan. He was the one I expected to stand up to them, telling them the entire thing was ridiculous. "What happens if I don't go?"

The Queen walked over to me and pressed her index finger onto the middle of my forehead.

She extended her other hand, and pressed her other index finger onto the middle of Tristan's forehead.

"What are you doing?" I asked.

"Checking the validity of this favor. Then, I can answer your question," she said.

The point of her touch was warm, sending little bursts of heat across my forehead. They were mild, and thankfully didn't hurt. The Queen held her finger on my forehead for a few more seconds, then slowly she moved her hands away from the two of us.

I glanced over at Tristan to catch him grinning. He looked as if this whole thing was going exactly as he had hoped. I really wanted to know what he was thinking. Why couldn't I read minds? It would make everything so much easier.

"You're favor bound," she said. "None of us would expect anything less from a Winter Fae, especially not *this* Winter Fae."

"What does that mean?" I asked.

"It means that you have to do this," she said.

"And if I don't?" I asked.

"You don't have a choice. The favor has been called in, you have a day to oblige or your magic becomes his."

"What?" I glared at Tristan. "What game are you playing?"

"No game, I'm simply cashing in what is owed to me."

Heat rose to my cheeks as anger swirled inside me. I couldn't believe that I'd started to think that he wasn't so bad. I'd even felt sorry for him when he shared the memory of his test. After everything, how could Tristan do this to me? And why would he do it now?

I turned to look at the others. They knew I had a favor with Tristan. They could have prepared me. "You all knew this, and no one said anything to me."

"We've been a little busy, love," Dane said.

"Maybe there are some of us who were hoping he wouldn't call upon the favor," Ethan said.

"So all of this conversation has been for nothing. I have no choice in this." I glanced at Tristan; he was still grinning. "Why now? Why do this to me now?"

"I told you I would help you, I fulfilled my end of the bargain. Don't you think it's fair that you fulfill yours?" Tristan asked.

I wanted to scream at him. I wanted to stomp my feet and tell them how unfair he was being. My face heated at the childish reaction that was flashing through my mind. I was a candidate for Queen's Trial. I was better than that. If nobody else was acting out of anger, I'd hold my tongue, too.

I was the only one in the room who wore any expression of emotion on my face. The others were standing by stoically, accepting my punishment with grace. I took a deep breath. I'd made this deal. This was my burden to carry and if I played his game, maybe he'd release me sooner. "Three weeks, alone, with you?" I asked Tristan, hoping it wouldn't be five.

"We won't be alone, Princess. The guards will be there, along with my advisors and the others who live in the palace. Perhaps some of my siblings will visit and keep you company," Tristan said.

I looked at Cormac one more time, he was my last hope of finding a way out of this. "And you're okay with this?"

Cormac glanced at Tristan, then turned back to me. "You're still under my protection. And you're linked with Ethan. If he does anything to upset you, we'll come for him. If he hurts you, I'll kill him."

Chapter Two

"If I have a day before I have to go, I'm not ready to leave just yet," I said.

"What did you have in mind?" the Queen asked.

"I came here for help with my magic. I don't want to continue to attract monsters. I need help."

She nodded. "You do. Nobody should have the powers you have. I don't even think the Queen should, now that I've experienced them." She frowned. "It's a large burden for anyone."

"Can you help me with that part? It's not help with the trials," I said.

"It really would be considered a safety issue," Dane said.

I smiled at him. "That's true."

"We probably have a few more hours before word of your arrival spreads," she said.

"Your staff is more loyal than mine, then," Tristan said. "Word would be out already if it were the Winter Court."

I scowled at him. "And that's where you want to take me? To a place where everyone will know I'm there so they can attack me again?"

He shrugged. "I told you, you'll be safe. Besides, the assassin was after me."

"Things are falling apart in your court, it seems," the Queen said.

"It's not my court, technically," Tristan said.

"That father of yours is still around?" the Queen asked, eyebrow raised in surprise.

"Don't worry, you'll receive an invitation to his funeral when the time comes," Tristan said.

"As much as I'd enjoy hearing about the turmoil of the Winter Court, Cassia is running out of time. Unless you're revoking the favor?" Cormac asked.

Tristan grinned. "You should get going, Cassia. Time moves quickly when you're on a deadline."

I glared at Tristan. I wanted him to know exactly how I felt about him calling in his favor now. He had to know exactly how he was upsetting my life. Was this his plan the whole time? Had he seen this in my future?

"General," the Queen called.

The door opened and the General popped his head in, then inclined his chin. "Your Majesty?"

"Please escort my guests to my receiving room. I'll be with them shortly," she said.

The princes filed out of the room, each giving me a wave or in the case of Tristan, a wink, on their way out.

My jaw was still tight from the anger I felt toward the Winter Prince. I couldn't prove it, but I had a feeling he planned this from our first meeting.

The door closed behind the others and I was alone with the Queen in her private, secret place. If she was correct, we'd have a few hours before one of her staff would leak that she was here with me. I already had enough of a reputation from traveling with four princes that I was seen as a threat. What was going to happen when word got out that I'd spent time alone with the Queen?

"Deep breath," she said. "In... out. Tristan is gone for now, it's just us."

Heeding her instructions, I breathed deeply and released the breath. I looked around the empty room and felt some of the tension I was feeling leave my shoulders and jaw. I didn't know the Queen, but she was my mother. And she'd cared about me enough to send me away so I had a chance to survive. Nothing in her plans had gone the way she wanted them to, but I was alive and that was incredible. Though, I knew I wasn't out of the woods yet. Tiana was after me and if my captors in the Winter Court were any indication of what was ahead for me in Queen's Trial, I had a lot of difficulty ahead.

"Thank you," I said. "I don't think I said that before. For saving me and hiding me."

She smiled, then settled into one of the chairs. "I wish I could have kept you, but it wasn't possible. And as much as I'd like to be a mother to you, I never can be."

I settled into the chair next to her. "What happens after Queen's Trial? What happens to you? Cormac told me the last Queen was one of Tristan's sisters."

"They didn't tell you?" she asked.

I shook my head.

"When a Queen's reign in finished, she returns to the temple and offers her magic to the gods."

"What does that mean?" I asked.

"It means, I'll surrender the magic I have once my reign is over and I'll return to where I was before becoming Queen unless the gods have something else in store for me."

"Like what?" I asked, a chill rippling down my spine.

"It varies from Queen to Queen. Most are granted a return to their old magic and some are stripped entirely." She rested her hands on her lap as if none of the words bothered her.

"So you could lose your magic?" From the reaction the others gave when I was put against the same threat by not following through with my favor bond, I figured it was a bad thing. So far, my magic had gotten me into a lot of trouble, but it had also saved my life on more than one occasion. "Is it worth it?"

"There isn't a choice in the matter, Cassia," she said. "A Queen reigns for one hundred years. Then, her time is up."

I leaned back in the chair and considered her words. I'd already signed up for this without having all the details. I didn't feel like I had a choice, that was for sure, but I didn't know it was a hundred year reign with a possibility of losing your magic once you stepped down.

"Now you know why it's such a problem for you to have all four courts worth of magic. Even past Queens don't have that," she said.

"What happens to the past Queens? Aren't the Fae immortal?" I asked, almost afraid of hearing the answer.

"Many of them go on living with their consorts and some of them even go on to have children after their reign. You can have a very happy life after serving as Queen." She lifted her brows. "And it is service. You work for the kingdom first. Your needs are second."

"And what happens to the Queens who don't go to live happy lives after their reign?" I asked.

She pulled her lips in tight and blinked a few times. "I don't want to discuss them. It's not up to us. The gods make the choice. It's impossible to know how your reign will end."

It was silent for a few moments and I played with the frayed end of the fabric on my sleeves. I wanted to be more afraid of what might happen to me if I were to become Queen, but the idea still seemed so absurd, that I wasn't sure how to feel fear. I wondered if I should worry. But a hundred years was a good, long life based on what I'd been raised to believe. It was beyond anything I'd expected growing up in the human realm and it was difficult to imagine that I'd need a longer life than that. I looked back up at the Queen. "Are you afraid?"

She shook her head. "Not for myself."

"For me?" I asked.

"Yes," she said, softly. "I'm very afraid for you. If you don't win, you won't survive beyond the new Queen's coronation."

My chest tightened in fear. While I couldn't find it in me to fear what might come after winning Queen's Trial, I was afraid of what might happen if I didn't win. "Do you think I stand a chance?"

"Maybe," she said. "If you can learn how to use the magic you have within."

"How will I do that while I'm stuck in the Winter Court?" I asked.

"Tell me about your test," she said. "What did Tiana find?"

I shuddered at the mention of the Queen's sister.

"Don't worry, she'll be punished when she reappears," the Queen said.

I tried not to worry about the fact that Tiana was out there, possibly waiting for me to be alone long enough to take me down. Maybe there was something good about being in the Winter Court. Tristan had no love for the Queen's sister. If she came into his home, he'd likely use the excuse to eliminate her. I had a feeling her punishment wouldn't be nearly as permanent if she were to return to the palace at the Autumn Court.

I took a deep breath and thought about the test, trying to recall each step. "She started with Summer. I turned the green strands into fire. Then, she tried Winter and I sort of went into her memories." I looked up at the Queen for reassurance.

She lifted an eyebrow. "You did? Well, I'm sure that surprised her."

"She wasn't happy about it," I said. "She accused me of being sent by someone. She thought I was out to get her."

"That sounds like her. What happened with the last two?" she asked.

"When she did Spring, I created pink flowers and with Autumn, I was nearly invisible. At least that's what she said."

"Stealth," the Queen said, then she laughed. "I've never heard of a Fae who could blend in with their environment to the point of invisibility, but it makes me think I might know who your father is."

"Oh?" I asked, straightening. I hadn't expected her to offer any information about my father after how quickly she dismissed it before.

"Your Winter magic is more skilled than I expected. Memory magic is tricky, and rare. Then, there's your Autumn magic. It's clearly your strongest point." She rested her finger on her chin. "It so happens that one of my consorts is half Autumn and half Winter. Logically, he'd be the most likely to be your father."

"I heard you have three consorts," I said.

She nodded. "Most Queens take multiple king consorts. We have a difficult job and it is nice to have extra support. Plus, with as much as we travel to all the realms, it's hard not to feel a mating bond with more than one Fae."

Flutters rose in the pit of my stomach as I thought of my princes. Was it possible I'd feel a mating bond with all of them? Would they stay with me if I were to win the trial?

The Queen stood. "We aren't here to discuss males, though, are we?"

I leapt from my seat. "No, we're not."

"We have a limited amount of time for you to learn how to control that magic you have so we better use our time wisely."

Chapter Three

"I can't teach you how to use all of your magic," the Queen said. "We don't have time for that. We'd need years. So we have to be smart about this. Tell me what you can do so far."

"Not much, honestly," I said. "I've been able to create a white light that blinds anyone around me and I was able to do some healing."

"And what did Cormac say about all of this?" she asked.

"He didn't really know what the white light meant other than it was how I was showing my untrained magic. He seemed more worried than anything else. He tried to teach me how to cycle."

"How did that go?" she asked.

"I got as far as learning how to find the magic internally, but I'm still not sure of what I should be doing with all of this information," I admitted.

"It's a lot," she said. "If you'd been raised here, you would have likely shown small signs and been trained a little bit at a time while you were a child to help you maintain control. Then, when you were of age, you'd have gone to the academy." She paused. "Though, I have no idea how magic of all four courts would have manifested in someone so young."

"What happens to other young Fae who have more than one court worth of magic?" I asked, trying not to let on that I knew someone who fit that description.

"That's a very rare thing," she said. "But it is worth exploring. That might be a good thing to ask one of your consorts to research for you. It could help you when it comes to the physical trials."

"Physical trials?" I asked, spikes of anxiety rising inside me. The more I heard about the trials, the more I was regretting agreeing to them.

"That's not our concern now. You won't even have to deal with them if you don't make it through the first three trials. So that is our focus. Keeping you alive through those."

"I like the idea of staying alive," I said.

The Queen smiled. "Let's focus on that, then. Cormac had the right idea about teaching you to cycle, but it's different with so much magic. With cycling, you want to keep it bubbling under the surface at all times so it's ready, but not in use. That's not possible for us. We can't turn it down low enough to not draw attention to ourselves from the creatures of the Under - or anyone else who is trying to detect magic for that matter."

"So what do I need to do?" I asked.

"You have to use your magic. You'll recharge much faster than other Fae, but if you don't use it, you'll carry around an active magical signature all the time."

"How often do I have to use it and how would I even begin that?" I was already feeling overwhelmed and we hadn't even started anything. All I could do was make a useless white light. It wasn't anything special or interesting. Sure, it had saved me a few times, but I figured that was more from luck than skill.

"Your Autumn magic is your most powerful so it will recharge the fastest. It's also going to be the magic that makes you easiest to trace so we'll start there," she said. "Tell me what you know about Autumn magic."

I thought back to my conversations with Cormac and how I'd bonded with him over our love of animals. Then, I thought about Angela and her suggestion to kill me. In the end, she'd asked Cormac to teach me how to track, which he'd started before we ended up in the Winter Court. I wondered if the Queen would want to know about Angela. I opened my mouth to tell her, then decided against it. She hadn't even seemed bothered by Tiana trying to kill me. Instead, I kept to the facts. "Hunting, tracking, animals." I paused as Tristan's comments about Cormac as a warrior struck me. "Fighting, perhaps, in wars."

She seemed pleased by my answers, nodded in agreement. "That is true, to a point. Yes, hunting and tracking and an affinity for all creatures. Which makes them excellent soldiers and fighters."

"How am I supposed to use that kind of magic?" I asked. "I don't have anything to hunt or track."

"First, I'd recommend you find an animal companion. I'm guessing you felt a connection to animals in the human realm, too?" she asked.

"Yes," I said. "Horses. They were my solace there."

"That makes sense. Having regular interactions with animals is going to allow you to use your magic without even realizing you're doing so. You'll be able to relate to the creature in a different way than others can. When you get to the Winter Court, ask for a horse. I'm sure Tristan will oblige."

I frowned. For a few minutes, I'd forgotten that my time with the Queen was very limited. I'd be in the Winter Court with Tristan by tonight. "I wish I didn't have to go."

"I know, but even if you weren't going with him, you couldn't stay here with me. You know that."

I nodded. "I'd rather be almost anywhere than trapped alone with him for weeks."

"You'll find a way to make the best of it, I'm sure," she said. "If you can find it in you to work with him, you might be able to study some Winter magic. There are few who practice it in Faerie since the kingdom's split."

"He'd probably ask me for another favor if I asked him to help me," I grumbled.

"You learned your lesson the hard way," she said. "I doubt you'll make that mistake again, am I correct?"

"I won't be making favors with anyone after this. It's not worth it." As soon as the words left my lips, I wondered if that were true. If I hadn't made the agreement with Tristan, what would have become of the other princes during that Sodalis attack? Would they have succeeded in taking them down on their own? I shuddered as I realized it was possible that Ethan might not have survived. I knew if I had to do it again, I wouldn't change anything. For better or worse, I was going to have to pay my debt. At least now, I could go into it knowing the price I paid for Ethan's life wasn't too high. I would have done far more to keep him living.

"Aside from having an animal companion, what else can I do?" I asked, changing the subject back to magic.

The Queen rose from her seat and took a step closer to me. I mirrored her movements, rising from my own seat and taking a step closer to her.

"Learning to harness and control the magic of all four courts is not something that can be taught." She extended a hand, giving a slight nod of encouragement. "It would be easier for me to show you. But you cannot speak of this to anyone, for it is forbidden for anyone who is not yet Queen to travel inside the sacred temple. If anyone finds out that I took you there, both of our lives are at risk."

Tentatively, I set my hand in hers. "Are you sure you want to do this then?"

She nodded. "As I said, it's the only way. Controlling magic of all the courts is something you feel at your core. It has to be experienced."

"I swear, I'll never speak a word of it."

The Queen closed her fingers around my hand. Then, I felt the tug of sliding in my gut as the air around me seemed to vanish, leaving us in a vacuum. I should be used to sliding by now, but the sensation still caught me off guard. I felt weightless as we floated through and I tried my best to keep the panic from rising inside of me.

I knew the darkness and the feeling of dread would pass as soon as our feet touched on solid ground, but it was still an uncomfortable sensation. As always, I blew out a breath of relief as my feet made contact with something solid.

Opening my eyes, I looked around. I couldn't tell where we were, everything was dark and I narrowed my eyes, squinting into the void. A heartbeat later, torches breathed to life in a rush of heat, filling the space with a warm flickering light. I gasped as I looked around at the interior of what appeared to be a cave. Dark, rocky walls surrounded me on all sides. Damp air cooled my skin and I breathed in the distant scent of moss and wet stone. Somewhere in the distance I heard dripping and I wondered if there were rivers that ran through the stone.

I thought we were going to the temple but I had never seen a temple like this. My visits to the human temple had been limited to the rare feast days when my father actually thought that showing up might bring him some accolades. If it didn't directly benefit him, my father avoided anything religious. He wasn't a believer and thought it was all a waste of time, though he never let anyone outside his home know he felt that way.

I enjoyed the time we went to the temples. Even if I was unsure about the gods, the spaces felt sacred and magical. I loved the large stone structures with their elegant rows of colonnades and thatched roofs. I loved the sculptures of the gods and goddesses and the smell of fresh flowers and ripe fruit that people brought for offerings. The human temples were a celebration of life. If this was a Fae temple, it held the opposite effect. The earthy scent and below ground damp made me think of death. It was more tomb than temple.

The Queen let go of my hand and traveled deeper into the space. As she moved, new torches lit in anticipation of her arrival. It was as if her body crossing through was enough to light the fire. I wasn't sure if it was a reaction of her role as Queen, or if any presence here would cause them to light, or if it was something she was doing with her own magic. Even though I had magic of my own, it still fascinated me to see it in action.

The Queen didn't show any signs of slowing down to wait for me to follow her. Wordlessly, I caught up to her and made sure I stayed a few steps behind her. The cave was full of tunnels, twists and turns that would be impossible to navigate unless you already knew your way around. I had a feeling that if I lost sight of the Queen for even a second, I might not know how to find my way back out of here. That terrifying thought was enough to keep me completely focused on where she was at all times. I wanted to look around more, see if I could catch sight of anything down any of the other tunnels, but I was too nervous to take my eyes off the back of the Queen.

She turned three more times, each time taking us deeper, and lower into the system of caves that we had entered. With every turn, the temperature dropped. I wrapped my arms over my chest and rubbed my hands up and down over my cold upper arms. I expected to see polished marble and priests and tablets and books of ancient promises and stories. I hadn't expected to be alone in a series of tunnels that seemed to travel nowhere.

Clearly, that wasn't the case, there was a destination ahead. Otherwise, it wouldn't be so well lit with all these torches. But the longer we walked, the more I began to wonder if the temple even existed. Was it possible this place was just a decoy, was there something else she actually wanted to show me? I shook my head, feeling foolish. There was no reason for her to trick me. But that was what I had thought about Tiana. I clenched my jaw, feeling guilty for not trusting the Queen. She was my mother and she'd saved my life. But the more time I spent in Faerie, the more I knew things weren't always as they seemed.

As soon as I turned the corner I froze. We were standing in a new chamber in the caves but this one didn't look anything like the dark tunnels we had been walking through. Every surface of the cavern was covered in sparkling gemstones. They twinkled and flickered in response to the mounted torches. It was a room of starlight. As if the night sky came here to rest during the day.

I took a couple of steps in and turned in a slow circle, admiring the glimmering cavern. I knew this was the place she'd been leading me to and as I took in the room, I felt more at ease. This was a truly sacred place. Even the air changed. It was clean and crisp, and had the lingering scent of grass and sunshine. How this place, buried deep underground in a damp cave could hold such wonder was beyond imagination. I had thought the human temples were beautiful, but they were built by man. This place had to have been placed here by the gods themselves. "It's beautiful."

"Yes," the Queen said. "It's said this room was built by the goddess herself as a place for her to take refuge when she visits our realm. Only the high priest and the Queen may visit this chamber. This is where the Queen comes after her coronation to obtain the magic of all four courts."

Against one wall, I noticed symbols carved deep into the stone. Below them was a small alcove where four small boxes were tucked inside protectively, as if being embraced by the stone itself.

"You found the incantations." The Queen moved over toward the boxes and gestured to them. "Each court of magic is linked to sacred stone, one stone for each box." She gestured upward toward the symbols on the wall. "This is the spell that is used to activate them. It's written in the sacred language, something you will learn if you win the trials."

"What happens if I win? Is it different since I already have the magic of all the courts?" I asked.

"I'm not sure," the Queen said. "Queen's Trial is an ancient right. And Queens weren't always forbidden from having children. My guess is that if you were to win, you would not be the first natural born with all of these powers."

I looked up, thinking about the Queen's words and giving myself a moment to process. Even the high ceiling of this cavern was covered in sparkling gems. I looked back down at the Queen. "If it wasn't always forbidden, I'm guessing something happened. Something bad."

"Yes." She walked away from the boxes and moved to the center of the cavern. "Long ago, one of the candidates who lost was naturally born with all four powers. She overthrew the winner of Queen's Trial, claiming the kingdom for herself. It was a dark time in our history and isn't known widely. The events are nearly forgotten, but the story is told every year when the final candidates move into the palace. Part of the final training is learning the history of Queen's Trial including the things that are better left forgotten."

"So that's why you say I have to win. After a story like that, there's no way I won't be seen as a threat. Unless they don't know about the magic I have. Can't I just keep it hidden?"

"It's not that simple," the Queen said. "Once you learn how to use your magic, you'll find it harder to ignore things that you use to not notice. The females that make it to the highest level for competing will be smart and savage. If they don't figure out your powers, they'll figure out your heritage and then work the rest out. Even if we don't say a word, there's always a way to find out what you want to know." The Queen extended her hand and summoned me by bending her fingers. "Now, come. This is what I brought you here for."

I walked over to where she was standing in the center of the cave. As I reached her, I walked through what felt like an invisible waterfall, a force that filled my entire body with ice cold making my eyes widen, and my breath hitch. I looked behind me, for any sign of what had caused such a disruption but saw nothing visible that might have caused me to feel that sensation.

Stretching my fingers out from the direction I had come, I reached until they brushed against something cold that flowed like water. When I pulled my hand back, my fingers were dry. My brow furrowed as I tested it again. It reminded me of the invisible barrier I had walked through between the Winter kingdom and Autumn Court. I turned back to the Queen. "What is that?"

"We've entered the sacred circle," she said, extending her arms on both sides of her. "Only those who have obtained magic from all four courts are able to cross. It's here you'll find what you're looking for."

Chapter Four

⚜

The ground began to vibrate under my feet and I tried to step away from the uncomfortable sensation, but it was as if my feet were locked in place, connected to the ground. I looked at the Queen, startled.

"Don't think, just feel," she said.

I tried to release icy tendrils of fear that were slithering over my skin. Feigning calm, I took slow breaths trying to ignore the tremors being sent as little shockwaves through my legs from the ground. The vibrations grew, increasing in both speed and intensity. I clenched my teeth and balled my hands into fists, my nails biting into my palms. It felt like all of my bones were shaking as this charge coursed through me. The feeling was somewhere between a tingling and tapping, and left me feeling both uncomfortable and out of control.

I'd come to learn that lack of control was one of the things that drove me to make a change. I wanted the freedom and the ability to do what I wanted to do. Right now, whatever was happening was preventing me from moving away from it. Heat rose in the pit of my stomach, a sense of rage bubbling against the restraints. I wanted to break free of this; I wanted to run away from these caves. Maybe even back to the human realm where things were comfortable and familiar. The thought startled me and I clenched my fists tighter, fighting the urge to flee.

I knew I didn't actually want to run. I knew there was nothing left for me in the human realm. My future was here, with magic. I belonged here. Even if the female in front of me was a stranger, she was my mother and she'd protected me. Plus, there were my princes. Now that I'd come to know them, I knew I could never walk away from them.

Some of the tension released, I was able to focus a bit more clearly on my surroundings. The circle we were standing inside was glowing I wasn't sure if that was new, or if I just hadn't noticed before. Either way, it was unusual, but also beautiful. The anger that had come on me so quickly, was subsiding like a breeze blowing away a pile of dirt. Now, I felt tears welling up in my eyes as an overwhelming sense of gratitude took me.

I'd survived against incredible odds, I was alive because of the fact standing in front of me, I might not know who I was, or how to do the things I should know how to do, or how to make sense of the fact that I'd fallen in love with three princes, but I knew each one of those things was precious. My heart swelled at the thought of the support I had and I smiled, realizing I had admitted to myself how I felt about each of the three of them. I loved them. All of them. And they were part of me just as I was part of them. My heart ached as I felt the overwhelming love I held for them swell within me. It was so intense, it frightened me. How was I supposed to react to a love so strong?

Just then, intense pain shot down my spine, forcing all thoughts from my mind. I fell to my knees, screaming in agony as the pain wrapped its way around my ribs, gripping me tighter. Each breath I took sent a shockwave down my chest and tears streamed from my eyes. Was I being punished for being here? Was I going to die here?

Finally, breathing grew easier and the pain subsided. Covered in sweat and still shaking from the experience, I tried to stand. The floor had released my feet when I fell but now my knees were locked in place.

I looked up for the Queen, reaching out my hand for her help. But she was gone. It was just me standing in a circle alone. I opened my mouth to cry out, but no sound came from my voice.

The pain returned in a rush, squeezing agony around my rib cage and I winced, bracing myself against it. The lights in the cave started to go out. One by one, the torches were extinguished and when the last one died, all of the glitter and sparkling gems became invisible, leaving me alone in the dark.

The grip around my ribs eased and I fell to my side, finally free from the hold of the stone below me. The pain had released, but now fear took hold. I was alone, in the dark, and terrified. My heart raced, and my palms were damp with sweat. I crawled on my hands and knees toward where I had last seen the Queen and reached a tentative hand, but found nothing but air. "Is anyone there?" I asked, my voice shaky now that it had returned.

No one answered, but I seemed to have gotten a response nonetheless. Out of the corner of my eye I caught sight of a faint glow. I turned to see a warm glow coming from each of the boxes that held the stones for each of the courts. Slowly, I pushed myself to standing, unsteady on my own two feet. Tentatively I took a step, surprised that I was allowed the freedom to move. I walked toward the boxes and looked at them quite a while before deciding that I needed to open one.

I studied them closely, noting the different colors. Green, gold, pink, and silver. One box for each court. My hand hovered over the gold box, knowing it held the magic of the Autumn Court, my mother's court. This was the magic that I should be strongest in, the magic I would've been born with had my mother not been Queen. What would my life have been like if she had just met my father and lived as a normal Fae? What if she had never signed up for Queen's Trial? What if I had grown up here?

Would I have been happy? Would I have felt as if I belonged from the very beginning?

A Nagging voice in the back of my head told me I wouldn't be who I was today if that were the case. If she hadn't hidden me away, it was possible I would have never met the princes. I didn't know for sure, but I knew I wasn't willing to go back to a time where none of them existed as part of my life.

I lowered my hand, not wanting to open the Autumn box. It seemed to speak of what could have been and I knew I had to move forward. Dwelling on the past, on what might have been wasn't going to help me.

Glancing at the other four, I wondered which I should open. Spring for my beloved Ethan? The healing magic I had been able to tap into to save him was invaluable. Or should I open Summer, learn more about the heat of passion that drove Dane? Then my eyes rested on the last box, one representing the magic of the Winter Court. It was by far the most mysterious of the four. I'd learned that those with Winter magic could sometimes read minds or tap into memories or in the case of Tristan, share their memories.

I was about to be prisoner in the Winter Court in exchange for a simple favor. I should be furious with Tristan, should want nothing to do with him once my favor was repaid, yet I couldn't seem to break free of the hold he had on me. I was curious about the Winter Prince, and I knew that curiosity was dangerous, just like him. But of all the magics that were offered before me, I felt most drawn to the mystery of the Winter Court. It was the magic that would impact my immediate future the greatest. Slowly, I reached for the silver glowing box and lifted the lid.

As soon as my fingers brushed against the top of the box, the lid opened revealing a smooth, shiny, silver stone. It looked like a polished rock and didn't have the same glow that the exterior of the box did. I looked around again, hoping to find the Queen for some sort of indication as to what my next step was. She was still missing from the space. As I returned my focus to the shiny silver rock, I wondered if her absence was real. Perhaps the magic of this temple had hidden her from me and she was still there somewhere observing me.

I hoped that was the case, thinking that maybe if I did something wrong, she would speak up. Imagining that she was there to guide me if needed, gave me the confidence to allow my instinct to take over. Cormac had encouraged me to follow my instincts when we were chasing monsters. According to him, intuition was stronger with Autumn magic. Taking a deep breath, I pressed one fingertip onto the top of the stone feeling the smooth, cool texture for a brief second before lifting my hand away quickly, testing to see if anything happened.

I had dealt enough with magic in the last several days to be wary of it. I knew it was something you shouldn't take lightly and I knew it was something that could just as easily harm as it could do good. I waited for a moment and looked down at my finger. It seemed to be normal, touching the stone had no impact on me so far. Feeling braver, I reach my hand out again and wrapped my fingers around the stone, getting a good hold of it before gently lifting it out of the box.

It was heavier than I expected, taking effort for me to hold it despite its small size fitting easily in the palm of my hand. The surface was incredibly smooth and it was cold like ice. It was a fitting stone to represent the magic of the Winter Court. As the thought crossed my mind, the stone seemed to warm in my hand. The stone began to glow, giving off a puddle of light like a lantern.

I narrowed my eyes and lowered my face a bit closer to the rock so I could study it. Interestingly, I could see my reflection almost perfectly staring back at me. It was as if I were holding a tiny mirror. Suddenly, a small shock broke through the stone into my fingertips, but I didn't pull my hand away. Something told me this was what I was meant to do so I continued to stare at my reflection and then I closed my other hand around the rock, sandwiching it between both hands until it was completely encircled by my palms. For a moment everything in my head seem to spin and I felt as if I was turning in circles as fast as possible. I squeezed the stone tighter, not wanting to risk dropping it at the sensation even though I knew I was still standing still.

As the spinning sensation subsided, the room around me began to shift. The darkness bleeding away to reveal a well-lit sitting room. This was familiar, it reminded me of when Tristan had shown me his memory. Seeing as how I was holding the stone that was the embodiment of Winter magic, I supposed I could be inside anyone's memory.

I looked around the room I was standing in and realized I was alone. Wood paneled walls met a glossy wood floor. Dark red velvet curtains were drawn allowing sunlight to pour in through a series of large windows along one wall. Across from the windows was a double doorway and the doors were closed. The room had no furniture, just me standing in the center of it waiting for something.

Just then, the doors swung open and two guards in Winter uniforms entered the room taking positions on either side of the doors. Behind them, came four females in fine gowns. The fabric whispered across the floor as they walked into the room. Each female wearing one of the four colors that I had come to associate with each of the courts. One in gold, one in green, one in pink, and one in silver. The females in the dresses took position standing in a row with their backs to the windows. I moved to the side, getting against the other wall so I could watch them without interruption. As I stood waiting, the females adjusted their dresses smoothing wrinkles and tugging on sleeves until a sound from outside in the hall made them all stand at attention. I turned to see who the newcomer was. I was greeted by a slender, blonde female in a flowing silver gown. She didn't look older than the others, but in the way she carried herself I knew she had wisdom beyond theirs. As she entered, all of the waiting females dropped into low curtsies.

"Rise," the female in silver said.

The others stood and fixed their gazes on the speaker.

"Welcome to the Winter palace, today is the first day of the second part of Queen's Trial. You four have been selected out of the original twenty-four candidates to advance to this round. One of you will replace me as Queen. From this moment on, you are not friends. Any alliance you had prior to your arrival here should be dissolved. While I encourage fair play, there are no rules in Queen's Trial. You would be best served to use your skills to your advantage without worrying about how others will be affected. Queen's trial will separate you, showing us the true leader who is meant to rule the land. Being Queen is not an easy position. And only the strongest can survive wielding the magic of all four courts. I will be available for one hour each week to meet with each of you privately. Other than that, you are on your own." The Queen looked at all of the candidates, her gaze lingering on each of them for a few seconds before moving to the next. Then she spun on her heel, silver skirts swishing in her wake as she exited the room. The doors remained open, but none of the candidates moved. After what seemed like several long minutes, someone spoke. "I suppose that means we go back to our rooms?" I looked along the line to identify the speaker and had no trouble realizing that of all the candidates, my mother was the one who broke the silence.

The scene blurred then returned me to the same room. Only this time, there were two females. My mother, in trousers and a torn, bloody tunic was facing the other female. Her clothes were similar, and just as destroyed as my mother's. The second female was crying. My mother walked over to her and placed her hand on the other candidate's back. "It's going to be alright," she said. "You made it through. You can't give up now, Maya."

Maya sniffed and looked up at my mother. "Why would you

say that to me? If I quit, you have one less candidate in your way. One less threat to your crown."

"That's not how I want to win," she said. "You can't let her get to you. What she did had nothing to do with the trial. You did everything correctly. She's the one who should quit. We can't have a Queen on the throne who stoops to betrayal and hate to win her crown."

"I don't want this bad enough to die for it, Samira." Maya wiped her tears. "None of us are Queen yet and we've already seen candidates die. Why must they make this so brutal?"

"You know that every death has been because the candidate either wasn't paying attention, like Fawn in the woods. She shouldn't have gone off the trail. We were all warned." Samira, my mother, lifted the other female's chin. "Or they were sabotaged. We can't give in. Can you imagine what it would be like to live under her reign?"

Maya wiped her nose and nodded. The tears finally gone. "You're right."

"I know what they told us," Samira said. "But there is no reason to stoop to their level. One of us can win this without playing dirty."

"Why are you helping me?" Maya asked. "Not that I don't appreciate it, but you don't owe me anything."

"No, I don't," she said. "But I want what is best for all of us. And I could see you on that throne and I would celebrate your victory. You have integrity. And that matters most of all."

The room faded around me returning me to the dark cave. I could hear my breathing and feel my heart thundering in my chest. I looked down at the silver stone and my brow furrowed. *Why did it show me that?* I thought the Queen had brought me here to help me learn how to use my powers. Instead, I was getting memories long past that didn't help me at all.

The dizzy feeling returned, and I grabbed hold of the rock tighter and braced myself to keep from swaying. Taking slow, deliberate breaths, I prepared to see another memory. Maybe this one would show me how my mother had learned to control her Winter magic.

I was thrown into another room, this time it was a bedroom that I didn't recognize. A simple bed stood against one wall covered in luxurious fabrics. Across from the bed was a fireplace surrounded by a few chairs. At first, I thought I was alone in this room as I had been in the previous room, but a sound made me turn. My eyes widened in surprise as I realized I was looking at myself and I wasn't alone.

My cheeks heated and my muscles tensed as I watched a different version of me running my fingers through Cormac's long dark hair. Our mouths were pressed together our bodies pressed even tighter. We both still had our clothes on, but this was far too intimate a moment for anyone to be witnessing even if it was myself.

I turned away, trying to give this version of me some privacy. This wasn't a memory because this had never happened. I had never been with Cormac.

Flutters filled my stomach as a little voice in my head told me it wasn't because I didn't *want* to be with Cormac. I looked back at the couple and a small thrill ran through me as Cormac slid his hand up my tunic. I pressed my lips together trying to maintain control of myself as I grappled to discover what was happening. This wasn't the first time I had seen myself with someone I hadn't been with. Then it clicked, this wasn't a memory, this might be the future. As soon as that thought entered my mind, the scene faded and I found myself once again holding the stone in the middle of the dark cave.

Chapter Five

Quickly, I set the silver stone back into its box and moved my hands away from it. My breathing was heavy. I was conflicted about what I had just seen. Of course I was interested in Cormac, but he had always been so careful with me to keep me at arm's length. My fingers trembled as I guided the lid back on top of the box closing away the stone from the Winter Court. It hadn't shown me what I wanted. Instead, it had shown me two memories and a flash that might be my future. How was that supposed to help me learn how to harness my magic?

I wondered if I was missing something or if I was supposed to have selected one of the other stones. I turned to look at the three remaining boxes just as I was going to reach for one, they slid from view in the wall that had previously existed closed over them encasing them behind stone.

The ground trembled. I took a few steps back, away from the place where the boxes had been. Did I anger the goddess? Suddenly, light appeared in the room I turned just as the torches were relighting and once again, the cave was sparkling as if millions of stars danced above me and around me. Leaving me confused and reeling from what I had just seen.

"You can't share what you learned here today," the Queen's said. I turned to find her emerging from the shadows. As I had suspected, she'd likely been there the entire time.

"I don't think I learned anything," I said.

"You did, but sometimes the goddess speaks to us in ways that aren't so obvious. Whatever she intended for you to learn was passed on to you today."

I wasn't so sure about that. In fact, I worried that I had made the wrong choice and that my inexplicable fascination with Tristan, even after everything he'd done, was costing me more than I bargained for. I should've selected a different stone then maybe I would be standing here with answers instead of standing here feeling more helpless than I had before I arrived.

"Come," the Queen said. "I have one more thing to show you." She turned and walked out of the temple room back into the twisting tunnels of the cave.

I followed, feeling nothing but dread seeping in to my very core. My arms and legs felt heavy and my mind was foggy. What I had seen didn't make sense and wasn't going to help me. Disappointed in both myself and the situation, I resigned myself to focusing on whatever it was the Queen was showing me next. Perhaps there was still a way I could benefit from this excursion.

After several more twists and turns, a cool breeze blew past me and I inhaled the sweetness of fresh, clean air. Ahead, I could just make out the opening for the tunnel and with each step more and more sunlight filtered in, washing away the dark, damp, gloom of this place.

I followed the Queen out of the mouth of the cave, emerging into a grassy meadow surrounded on all sides by steep rock formations. We were in a valley surrounded by high, craggy mountains. The cave we'd come through seemed to be the only way in or out. How had anyone even found this place?

Soft green grass was dotted with white and red wildflowers. Somewhere nearby there was water as I could hear the gentle bubbling of the stream. If I were a goddess, this would be my sanctuary. Not that dark cave deep underground. No, I wouldn't want to be trapped under all that rock. I would want to be out here where I was free.

Sunlight warmed my skin and I could practically taste the sweetness of honeysuckle in the air. A gentle breeze rippled the fabric of my dress, reminding me that I was in the tattered and dirty remains of what I had worn when I fled from Tiana. Despite her regal appearance and her position, the Queen had never once flinched at how I was dressed. I had a feeling she was more like me than I could imagine and wasn't much impressed by exterior appearances; facades that some might don to impress her.

The Queen paused in front of the stone that was nearly as tall as her. It was part of many stones that formed a circle in the center of the meadow. These had not grown from the hills in this pattern accidentally, they were placed here. As I moved to her side, I joined her in quiet reflection. I felt the weight of this place. An honest and somber feeling settled over me as my eyes traveled across the spiral of tall rocks. This was a sacred place, an ancient place. Deep down, I knew I was one of the few who had ever seen it.

"When I die, the current Queen will bring my remains here and a new stone will be summoned for me. This is a place of great power and great contemplation. Every Queen since the beginning has been laid to rest here when her time comes to an end."

I stared at the circle of stones, in awe at the sheer number of them laid out in front of me. Dozens of Queens had ruled in Faerie. Each of them giving their time to rule and care for the lands I had just learned existed.

How was I going to pull this off? Even if I were to win whatever it was that was expected of me during Queen's Trial, how could I live up to these expectations? I had only just discovered I was Fae.

I felt small, overwhelmed and unworthy. "I don't even know

the first thing about Faerie, or how to use magic, or the traditions and expectations of this place." I could almost feel the accusations rising from the spirits of the Queens who had come before me. I felt like a fraud. "I shouldn't be here. I shouldn't be participating in Queen's Trial. Self-preservation isn't the reason you rise to become a leader."

"No, it's not," the Queen said. "But knowing that is not the reason, is one of the things that will give you strength. You weren't raised for this job. And in some ways that's a blessing. You will be able to look at problems with fresh eyes, unencumbered by the moral constructs and social institutions that have plagued Faerie for generations. That's why I hid you away."

"I thought you had me away so they wouldn't kill me," I said, confusion causing my brow to furrow.

The Queen turned and looked at me. "Any female who can control her magic is very good at understanding her body. I could feel you growing inside me within the first few days of conception. I could have stopped it right then and there, but I didn't. I'm not sure why I let it happen in the first place, but now I'm starting to think that maybe this was what I wanted all along. Maybe I hoped you would return. The Winter Court was the first to leave, but if something doesn't change, they won't be the last. If the four courts are severed, we will be weak and it will be easier for the creatures of the Under to find their way to us. There were dark times once before, in the times before the Queens. The creatures of the Under passed between worlds without care. We keep them in check now, sending our best warriors, like Cormac, to defend everyone. But if our borders are closed down the way they are between Faerie and the Winter Court, resources will dwindle and the Under will rise. We maintain balance and peace by working together. We were never meant to be divided."

"And you think I'm the one who's going to help keep the peace? I don't know anything about diplomacy."

"You spent the last several days getting Cormac and Tristan to travel together and work toward a common goal. You know how they feel about each other. Clearly, you have a gift for diplomacy," she said.

"That doesn't count." I shook my head. "Tristan was using me. He wanted something from me, he still does. He went along with it for his own purpose not because I compelled him to be nice to Cormac."

"You don't see it yet, how much power you actually have," she said. "But you will." She turned away from me, her gaze focusing back on the circle of stones in front of us.

I swallowed, and turned away from her to look at the reminder in front of me. These were the past, the legacy left by the Queens who had come before my mother. There was an energy vibrating around me and it made me feel connected to the very fabric of nature. I couldn't explain the sensation, but I welcomed it. I grappled with my thoughts, trying to think of words powerful enough to explain how this place made me feel.

My arms and legs hummed with gentle electricity, a charge that reminded me of the feeling I got right before I used my magic. Only this time, it wasn't clawing, it wasn't painful. It was ever present, and somehow soothing. I wondered if that was how magic was supposed to feel. I closed my eyes and took a deep breath, forcing the sensation to memory. I wanted to take this back with me, every emotion, every thought, every sensation. I knew this was meant to be a lesson and I wanted to learn.

Slowly, I opened my eyes and glanced over at the Queen. She was looking at me again, a smile on her lips. "You can feel it, can't you?"

I nodded.

"We should get back," she said. "Speak of what you've seen to no one. But think on it often, as these are the best lessons I can give you. When we return, we will not be able to speak again until you make it back in the top four. And even then, all of our conversations must be in an official capacity."

I nodded, my heart already aching at the thought of departure. I'd been so lonely in the human realm, even when I was surrounded by people. With my newfound companions, that ache in my chest had vanished, replaced by a sense of fulfillment and peace. The thought of leaving them behind to return to the frozen Winter Court left me feeling hollow.

The Queen began to walk toward the cave and I followed with heavy footsteps. The Queen paused in front of the entrance to the cave. "Stay close, as soon as we are out of the sacred space, we can slide back to the palace." Her tone was formal and stiff. Returning to the voice of a Queen to her subject rather than that of a mother to her daughter.

"Thank you. I know what you risked to do this. I won't let you down," I said.

"I know you won't." She turned away and stepped into the cave.

I followed behind her, feeling a strange sense of detachment from her. I felt like I was isolated, on an island of my own making, not quite fully immersed in any one place.

Chapter Six

❧❧❧

I sat alone in the guest bedroom I had been taken to. My whole
life had become a series of travels from one place to the next
without ever getting an opportunity to be comfortable where I
was before I had to pack up and leave once again.

I nearly laughed at my own musings as I realized that in order
to pack up, I would need to have some belongings of my own. I
had nothing. I came to the Fae realm with nothing, and while I
had gained friendship and love and a better sense of who I was, I
was nearly as confused as I had been when I arrived. What was to
become of me now?

Did I actually have the ability to compete against these
females who had been raised from birth for the job of Queen? If
the situation were reversed, and I was the one who expected to
fight for this title that I had been raised for, that I had dreamed
about, being groomed for since birth, I would not be happy to see
an offspring of the current Queen entering the competition. I
would feel betrayed, and hostile toward the stranger who knew
nothing of our ways.

I'd seen it before, the whispers and stares directed toward my
human family from those who had money for generations. New

money was never taken seriously and was often looked at as a threat.

I wasn't new money here exactly, but it had to be something similar. Shaking my head, I tried to harness the peace and power of the valley my mother had taken me to. She believed in me and I was safe for now.

I straightened my shoulders and pushed the dark thoughts away. I'd been through too much and come too far to give up now. The other candidates wouldn't even meet me until we got to the top four. By then, I'd have proven myself with the first three trials, whatever they were. I'd have to make myself shine. I'd have to find a way to prove I belonged here. I might not know much about the history or culture of Faerie yet, but I had time.

Forcing what I hoped was a determined expression on my face, I marched toward the door and stepped into the hallway. A guard greeted me by inclining his head. "What can I do for you, my Lady?"

Lifting my chin, I worked to affect the heir of importance I thought matched the title he was using to address me. "I'd like to see the Autumn Prince. Can you take me to him?"

Of all my companions, the one who had the best understanding of court life was Cormac. If I was going to learn how to act the part, he was the one who could teach me.

"This way, my Lady," the guard said with a gesture of his hand.

I followed him down a long hallway and continued my quiet contemplation. I'd sure seen the inside of enough palaces to last me a lifetime. If only the social climbing human who had claimed to be my father could see me now. He'd have given anything for a chance like this.

To be fair, he probably would've sacrificed Rose for a chance like this. I wondered how much he knew about the inner workings of the Fae. Had they told him anything other than the fact that they would pay him if they kept me alive? How he would be kicking himself now if he knew who I was and the chance that I had in front of me. Served him right, the man never cared for anyone or anything aside from money and status. And while money could be used to buy wonderful things, it meant nothing if you were alone.

With each step down the hall, my chest tightened with longing contrasted by occasional flutters of hope. I'd only been parted from the princes for a few hours, but seeing a familiar face and feeling a familiar embrace made my throat tighten with need.

How was I going to get through weeks without them when hours felt like days? We turned the corner and then turned another and I heard the sound of male voices growing louder as we approached. The tightness in my chest gave way to relief as I recognized both Cormac and Ethan's voices.

I bypassed the guard and picked up my pace to one that was probably too quick for a lady, but I didn't care. Happiness overtook me as I crossed the threshold. I came to a sudden stop as I caught sight of Tristan. I wasn't ready to deal with him yet.

Ethan was the first on his feet and the first to sweep me up in a hug. He lifted me, spinning in a circle as he pulled me so close to him I lost the ability to breathe for a moment. After setting me down he pressed his forehead against mine.

"You haven't even left yet and already I feel pain from your absence."

"I feel the same," I said. Then I lowered my voice. "Please tell me you worked something out and I don't really have to go."

He straightened, and let out a sigh. I searched his blue eyes for any sign of hope, but all I could find was reserved acceptance. He was going to let me go. They all were. I blinked back tears and swallowed hard, willing the emotion to leave my face. I brushed my fingers over Ethan's cheek and he caught my hand, pressing it against his face then pulling it to his mouth kissing my palm. Clasping my hand in his he lowered it. "It's only a few weeks, you'll be back before we all know it."

"Liar," I said, forcing a smirk on my lips.

Someone cleared their throat and I turned, startled. I'd forgotten that Ethan and I weren't alone. "Should we give you two some privacy?" Tristan asked.

I glared at him. "You could give me my life back."

"I'm not taking your life, princess. Just a couple of weeks of your knowledge. Have you forgotten that you're immortal? In the grand scheme of things it is hardly any time at all."

"How was your time with the Queen?" Cormac asked, seemingly unfazed by the drama playing out before him. "Did you get everything you needed?"

"I actually have some questions for you," I said. "Maybe we can talk?"

"Of course," he said.

Taking a deep breath I walked deeper into the room and settled onto the green velvet sofa. Ethan sat next to me and Cormac and Tristan settled into the sofa across from us.

"Don't you have anything better to do?" I asked, looking at Tristan.

"Not until we return to my castle," he said with a grin.

It took every ounce of my willpower to refrain from rolling my eyes at him. I had a feeling he enjoyed seeing how far he could push me. So I turned my attention to Cormac. "I want to know everything I can about the political structure, social habits, and culture of Faerie. If I'm going to make an attempt at becoming the Queen, I need to know what I'm the Queen of. It's not fair to any of the Fae who live here to have someone ruling them who doesn't even know their history. I didn't even know how weddings worked. I don't know anything of the structure of your religious system. I'm like a child here, and until I know those things, I have no place even pretending I should be the Queen."

Out of the corner of my eye I saw Tristan lean forward, resting his elbows on his knees. He looked completely interested in what I was saying.

"You're right," Cormac said. "You need to learn all those

things. But I don't think we'll have time to cover all of that before you go."

"Don't you see this is why I can't leave," I said, glancing at Tristan before returning my gaze to Cormac. "Everyone says I need to do this, but I'm not ready. If I'm wasting my time in the Winter Court, I'm not going to stand a chance. How can you just sit by and let him take me away like this?"

"Enough," Cormac said.

"No!" I jumped to my feet. "No. It's not enough. You all keep me in the dark and then you send me away and you don't even care. I'm sick of this and I don't want to be part of any of these games anymore."

"Enough!" Cormac yelled.

I've never heard him raise his voice and the sound startled me, causing me to freeze in place, eyes wide. My lower lip trembled as disappointment coursed through me. When I regained the ability to move, I shook my head at him. "No. Not enough. I expected more from you."

I turned and walked out of the room. If he wasn't going to help me, I'd look for a library. Somewhere I could get some answers. Or maybe I could find Dane. He was one of the only ones who would stand up to Cormac when he got this way.

"Cassia, wait," Cormac called.

I ignored him and continued walking down the hall. I could feel him behind, me but I didn't turn around.

"Cassia," he called again.

I stopped and turned to face him. "You can't keep everything from me. Hiding this from me is going to get me killed. How am I supposed to have a chance at this if I don't know what I'm up against?"

"I know," he said. "It's just that I don't want you to change."

My brow furrowed. "What do you mean?"

He sighed. "Your intentions and ideas are so pure. You come from a place of intuition and heart. You aren't letting anyone else influence your opinions. I've tried for years to get things to change around here and I'm always met by excuses about how we can't change because of tradition or because it's the way things are. You don't know how things are so you aren't locked in."

I took a step closer to him and touched his arm. "You're going to have to trust me."

"I know," he said, setting his hand on top of mine.

"Besides, I have something none of the others have." I reached for his face, gently lifting his chin so dark eyes met mine. "You as a moral compass to guide me. If I'm off track, you can help bring me back."

Cormac smiled and clasped my hand with both of his. Slowly, he lifted my hand to his lips and kissed me as if he were kissing a dignitary.

I looked away from him as disappointment sank into my gut. Biting down on my lower lip, I pulled my hand away from him. Every inch of my skin was on fire from his touch and I ached to be closer to him. Intimate with him. But he maintained his distance. Every time I thought I'd broken through, he pulled away.

"Have I upset you?" he asked.

I shook my head. "No. It's not you."

"I know I don't always do the right thing, Cassia, but I do care for you. Is it the information? We can talk right now. I'll tell you anything you want," he said.

I looked up at him through my lashes and I saw it: the want in his gaze. I'd seen it before, when we were alone in the stock yard. We'd had a moment before Tristan had torn it away from us.

My heart beat faster and flutters filled my chest. I knew he could feel the pull between us the same as I did. How was he resisting this so well? It was taking all of my willpower to keep my hands from finding their way under his tunic.

Breathing shallow, I took a few steps toward him, closing the gap between us. "It's not that, Cormac. I mean, I want to know all those things, but there's something else. Don't you feel it?"

Fear seized me as I waited, my half confession hanging between us.

"I'm no good for you, Cassia. You know I'd do anything to protect you, but you're better off spending your time with Ethan or Dane. I can't give you what you need."

"That's not true," I said. "If anything, I'm the one who isn't good enough for you. You're a prince. I'm just a changeling."

"You're going to be Queen," Cormac said. "Don't let anyone tell you otherwise."

I reached up and caressed his cheek with my palm, letting my fingers linger at his jaw. I felt him lean into my touch. "No more self-loathing. If it helps, consider that an order from your future Queen."

He smirked. "You're not Queen yet."

"No, I'm not," I agreed. "But with your help, I'm starting to believe I might be. And I insist on having you by my side. In every way possible."

Cormac was very still for a moment, then he sprang to life. Before I realized what he was doing, he had me in his arms, lifting me off the ground as he pressed his mouth against mine.

I wrapped my legs around his waist, kissing him hungrily while he walked down the hall. We tumbled into the first closed door we found and he threw me on a couch in an empty study.

My whole body was on fire with need and the place between my legs tingled in anticipation. I clenched my thighs together, unwilling to allow myself to believe anything was going to happen. It was too good and I never wanted it to end. Taking shallow breaths, I tried to steady myself as I looked up into those dark eyes, drinking in every inch of him.

In all the excitement, Cormac's hair had come loose of its usual plait down his back. Long, dark waves of hair hung loose around his face cascading down to his collar bone. He was breathing just as heavy as I was.

I wasn't sure if he was trying to restrain himself or if he was deciding how to make his next move on me. Either way, I was afraid that if I said anything, he'd walk away, leaving me here to wonder what could have been. I couldn't let him stop now. Weaving my fingers through his dark hair, I eased his head closer to mine, bracing myself for another kiss.

Chapter Seven

I pressed my mouth against Cormac's, hungry for the release of the tension I felt every time I was near him. Using my free hand, I grabbed hold of his upper arm digging my fingernails into his firm bicep.

Cormac pulled away from me, eyes wild, his breathing heavy. He smiled down at me, in a way that made him look like a predator about to devour his prey. His expression sent the slightest sense of alarm though me but it was quickly muffled by my want. The sensation of it sent a thrill through me that escalated into a tingling sensation low in my belly. I had never wanted someone more than I wanted Cormac.

I reached for him again, intending to pull him back to the kiss he'd broken but he pulled away, grabbing hold of both of my wrists in one of his large hands. Taking shallow breaths, I stared up at him, desperate for more. We seemed to be exchanging a silent conversation, unable to express our needs and desires with words. It was as if he was fighting the way he felt. Like an animal in heat trying to break free of the mating instinct.

I leaned forward, wrists still bound, and nipped at his earlobe.

Cormac let out a growl then buried his face into my neck then he traced his tongue along my neck, up to my ear where he returned the nip on my ear.

I gasped, suddenly aware of how sensitive every inch of my skin was. The fabric of my dress was making my nipples uncomfortable and I shifted, trying to reposition myself. I wanted to free myself of my clothing but when I tried to move my hands, Cormac's grip tightened. With my wrists still bound, I couldn't take charge. I felt deliciously trapped by Cormac's whim. It was frustrating and amazing at the same time.

I clenched my thighs together as the wetness between my legs increased. Every inch of me was on fire and I was desperate for release. "Please." The word came out as a whisper between heaving breaths.

Cormac lifted my wrists above my head and using his free hand, he unlaced the top of my dress. The fabric hung loose, resting just above my nipples but he didn't touch me.

I whined in disappointed frustration, making a sound that was more animal than I thought I could make. Before I could beg again, Cormac released my wrists. He lifted me off of him, leaving me in a breathless heap on the couch.

I held my breath, frozen in fear as he took a step away from where I was sprawled out on the couch. My brow furrowed. "Don't stop."

That was all he needed. In an instant, we was back in front of me, pulling me up to a sitting position. Then, he dropped to his knees and lifted my skirt until it was bunched up around my waist. He opened my knees, spreading them apart. I felt my cheeks heat as he kissed my inner thigh. His mouth worked its way up to my center and I felt the heat of his breath against me while he continued to kiss me over my undergarments.

My head rolled back against the couch and I moaned in pleasure. His fingers teased me, still over the thin layer of fabric and I moaned again. It wasn't enough for climax and the agony of waiting was making me whimper. I reached down to remove my undergarments, but Cormac caught my hands, lifting them over my head again.

"Not yet," he said.

"I want you," I said. "All of you."

"Not yet," he said again, grinning.

He released my hands, then slid his fingers up the bodice of my tunic until he reached my breasts. He started off gentle, slowly caressing my breasts working his way to the sensitive nipples. I yelped as he squeezed them at the same time. A rush of pain mingled with the pleasure of his touch as he went back to the gentle caress. I leaned into him, encouraging him to continue, desperate for more. He lifted the dress over my head, leaving my breasts exposed to him. His mouth was on me again, tongue flicking each sensitive nipple, before I had time to adjust to the chill in the air. I wove my fingers through his hair as I held the back of his head against my chest. He continued to work his tongue and mouth over my breasts until I arched my back in pleasure, letting out staggered breaths as the feeling built inside me.

Just as the pleasure was coming to a peak, Cormac pulled away then leaned over me, boxing me in with his arms on either side. He made me feel small, and I had forgotten how much larger he was than me. For a second, I felt the slightest fear trickle down my spine as I realized how much I was at his mercy. The place between my legs throbbed in want as I realized that I liked being in his control right now.

Cormac leaned down and pressed his lips against mine. He was hungry, aggressive, unrelenting as his tongue pushed into my mouth until it met mine. He pulled back on the kiss, then bit down on my lower lip just hard enough to send a flicker of pain with the pleasure. It was as if he knew how to walk a tightrope between the two, keeping the pleasure at the forefront while the pain was just enough to push me over the edge. My undergarments were soaked and I let out a moan as he pulled his mouth off of mine.

Cormac stepped back and kicked off his boots, then removed all of his clothing from his bottom half, releasing his erection.

My eyes widened at the sight of him exposed and truly vulnerable in front of me for the first time. But that thought didn't last long as I watched him grow right before my eyes to an even more impressive size. Nervous, I clenched my legs together, afraid my body wouldn't stretch to accommodate him.

Cormac laughed. "Now you're being shy?"

He charged back over to where I still sat on the couch and he picked me up as if I were nothing more than a doll and turned me so I was laying across the couch on my back. He lifted one of my legs so it was over the backrest and I instantly moved my hands down to cover myself, feeling more exposed than I had before.

Cormac rested his hand on top of mine, giving me a moment to react.

This was what I wanted. To be closer to him, to feel him inside me. My body ached for it.

I moved my hands away and reached for him, weaving my fingers into his long dark hair. He lowered himself onto me, and kissed my jaw and my neck my chin before his lips found mine again. He moved slowly this time, gently. The heat of the initial action had faded into something more intimate and personal. All of the animalistic desire was spent and now it was us. Cormac, my prince, finally willing to show me how he felt about me.

His tongue found his way into my mouth and mine greeted him eagerly, performing a dance of movement as our mouths became one. My back arched as his fingers found the sensitive nub between my thighs and I lifted my hips so he could remove my undergarments. His erection pressed against my inner thigh as he continued to use his fingers to send waves of pleasure through me. I moaned into his mouth as he slipped one of his fingers inside me, gently moving it in and out while his thumb maintained its exploration of the little nub.

He broke free of the kiss and stared down at me. The smile he wore now was sweet and free of the pain I so often saw him in. "I love you, Cassia."

I gasped, nearly speechless at the declaration. He didn't give me a chance to respond before his mouth was on mine again and his erection slid inside me.

Stars danced in my vision as he filled me completely. I broke free of his kiss as my head tipped back and I screamed in pleasure. All of the waiting, all of the teasing had kept me at the brink of climax and now it crashed over me in one giant wave.

Cormac continued to thrust into me and I grabbed hold of his back, digging my fingernails into his skin for support as I gasped for air. I never wanted this to end.

Chapter Eight

Tristan's palace seemed even larger than it had the first time I'd seen it. The rooms were empty and the chill of the Winter Court seeped into my bones. Now that I knew the Queen, an Autumn Fae, was my mother, I knew I had no Winter blood. My ability to enter the Winter Court must have come only from the powers I possessed.

"As long as you're here, you have free reign of whatever you need," Tristan said.

"Does that mean I can go back to the Autumn Court when I want to?" I asked, already missing the company of the princes I'd left behind.

"Nice try," he said. "You're here until you have completed your end of the bargain."

I shivered and wrapped my arms over my chest. "We both know this has nothing to do with your curiosity about humans."

He shrugged. "Perhaps."

I scowled at him. "I thought you were my friend."

"Didn't Cormac warn you? You shouldn't trust me," he said.

Two servants in blue walked into the room and lowered their heads in greeting. "Welcome home, Your Grace."

"Thank you," Tristan said. "Bella, see to it that Lady Cassia is taken care of. She'll be staying with us for a while."

"In the Princess suite?" Bella asked.

Tristan glanced at me and raised an eyebrow in silent question.

I narrowed my eyes and shook my head. Whatever this was, it wasn't my choice. I didn't want to be here to play house with him. I wanted to get back to the others.

Tristan turned away from me. "No, the grand guest room is fine."

"Are you sure?" Bella asked.

"I'm sure."

"Lady Cassia." Bella curtsied. "If you'll follow me."

"Shouldn't we start with the favor?" I asked. "I mean, don't I have twenty-four hours to show that I'm going to comply?"

"You just met your mother and haven't had a chance to rest since someone tried to kill you. I thought you might want to freshen up before we get to business." He looked me up and down. "Besides, you smell like the Autumn Prince."

My cheeks heated and I bit the inside of my lip to keep from saying anything. It wasn't like we'd tried to hide what we'd been doing before I left. I licked my lips, recalling the feel of Cormac's mouth on mine. It seemed like so long ago and I wanted so badly to get back to him, but I was going to have to be patient. I felt like saying something to anger Tristan, but it was going to be a long enough visit as it was. With a sigh, I collected myself. "Alright. Rest first. But after we discuss the questions you have, I have some of my own."

He lifted an eyebrow. "Another bargain?"

I shook my head. "No, no more bargains or favors. If we're going to do this, you have to start being at least a little nice to me. You took me away from the others right as I'm beginning Queen's Trial. I'm going to need your help."

"I never thought I'd hear you ask me for help as a friend,"

Tristan said. "I think you'll find that I can be civil. Kind, even, once you get to know me."

I pursed my lips. I'd seen those sides of Cormac. I'd seen the nice prince, the one who cared about others. I'd also seen the trickster and the shameless flirt. "We'll see."

Tristan inclined his head toward me and turned away. I watched him walk for a moment, feeling more confused than ever about him.

I followed Bella up the grand staircase and down the hallway into a part of Tristan's palace I hadn't seen during my last visit. We only stayed one night last time, so I'd seen the room that he put me in as well as a sitting area and a dining room. This time, I was being placed in a different wing of the palace. I wondered how big this place really was. Shivering again, I rubbed my palms on my arms to warm myself. Some clothing more suitable for this court would be nice to try and eliminate the chill.

We stopped in front of a door and the servant opened it for me inclining her head toward the room. "Would you like me to set up a bath, my Lady?"

I peeked into the room and saw a large four-poster bed, a few chairs around the fireplace, a dressing table and a wardrobe. It was a nice room, and there was room for a tub on the floor, but I couldn't help a flashback to the last time I took a bath in a room like this alone.

I stared at the window, sheer curtains filtered the sunlight and thicker curtains were pulled to the side. I wanted to cross the room and make sure it was locked, but that still might not be enough to get rid of the uncomfortable feeling that I wasn't safe. "I think I'll pass on the bath, thank you."

"I heard about what happened to you, about the attack. We know they were after someone else, but it must make you nervous to be alone. I can stay with you, or I can show you to the springs under the palace. They're harder to access and there are no windows," Bella said.

"Springs?" I had never heard of springs being used in place of a bath. We had spring water brought into the human town I'd grown up in. It was sold for ridiculously high prices and said to cure all sorts of ailments. I had never been to any of the pools that were supposed to contain this magical water. "That would be nice."

"This way, my Lady. I'll show you, then I can bring you fresh clothes."

I stepped away from the door, and Bella closed it behind me.

"Tristan won't mind?" I asked. He seemed rather set on sending to me to my room and I didn't want to get Bella in trouble.

"I doubt he'll mind. If you're important enough to stay the night in your own suites, I think he wants you to be comfortable. It's rare that he has guests that stay at all. Sure there's the occasional party or diplomatic visits. Sometimes they unintentionally stay the night, but they're never put up in a nice room. They all get the standard guest rooms. You're on the family floor. All the suites here are for royalty. We didn't get any warning about you, and there's going to be a lot of gossip, care to fill me in?"

I laughed, Bella's honesty was refreshing after dealing with Tristan. I liked her and I hoped that I would get to spend more time with her while I was stuck in the Winter Court. "I'll be here for a few weeks. Tristan and I have an arrangement, I owe him a favor, as it were. And until I pay it off, I will remain here."

I couldn't think of any reason why I shouldn't just tell her the truth, so I did. It was another first for me. Since arriving in Faerie, I had kept most of my true intentions to myself. There was something liberating about being honest.

"And here I thought you were the mysterious future princess we keep hearing about," Bella said.

My brow furrowed as a surprising rush of jealousy surged through me. "What do you mean?"

"Nothing," Bella said. "Just speculation among the staff. His

Grace sent orders a few days ago to prepare the princess suite. We've wondered if that meant he finally met someone. His heart was so broken after he lost his last mate. It would do all of us good to see him happy again."

"I'm sure," I said.

"Now tell me about this favor," Bella said. "You don't mean an actual favor with the Winter Prince, do you? I can't imagine anyone would make that mistake."

I winced, feeling the sting of her words. I'd come a long way since I made that bargain and I felt like I was a different Cassia than the Cassia who was foolish enough to strike that deal.

"I like you," I said. Bella didn't hold anything back, she reminded me of Lainey and I wondered how she was coping with the week off of work. Perhaps Tristan could send her to come here and keep me company. "But I've had a long day. I'd rather not talk about Tristan anymore."

We passed through the sitting room, and down the long hallway lined with portraits of tapestries. Bella stopped in front of another door and opened it. "I like you, too. And I hoped he was preparing that suite for you. We could use someone like you to keep him on his toes. He needs someone to stand up to him from time to time."

I smiled. "I do my best."

She gestured toward a set of stairs behind the door. "The springs are in the basement, and naturally heated so you'll feel warmer as you get closer. Only the royal family and distinguished visitors are allowed access so you should have some privacy."

I looked down the stairs, they were made of stone and lit by a strange orange glow coming from somewhere down below as the only light. It gave the illusion of walking right into the center of the earth. I shuddered and wondered if I should have stayed in my room. A strange smell filled the air. It reminded me of eggs left out too long.

"I'll return shortly, you won't be alone long," Bella said.

"Unless you'd like some company?" Tristan's voice came from behind me.

"Your Grace." Bella dipped into a curtsy.

"Leave us," Tristan said.

Bella curtsied again and scurried away, not looking back.

Tristan was alone. He never seemed to travel with guards the way he had made me do.

"I can go if I'm interrupting," I said.

"There's plenty of room, and I'll be on my best behavior," Tristan said. He extended his arm toward the doorway. "After you."

Part of me wanted to turn around and stomp back to the room I had been shown to, but there was also a flicker of curiosity that I couldn't quite extinguish. Tristan seemed to be in one of his good moods and he had let on that he'd try to be nice. Part of me longed to be near him, which startled me, but also drew me in closer.

I looked at the dark stairs again and back to Tristan. He was waiting calmly, giving me time to make the decision. He wasn't pushing me, or trying to convince me, or threatening me in any way. He was simply waiting. I knew from his expression that if I wanted to make a scene and run off, he wouldn't stop me. He was giving me a choice in this when he hadn't given me a choice in whether or not I wanted to come and spend time at his palace with him in the first place. I probably should've walked away, but the curiosity won and I lifted up my skirts so I could descend the stairs.

As Bella had said, the temperature increased with each step. It wasn't uncomfortable, but it was surprisingly warm. When I reached the bottom, I looked around the cave like space. Several pools of water were surrounded by uneven rock formations stretched as far as I could see.

Flickering torches lined the walls giving the space a warm, orange glow. Some of the pools were large enough for only one or two people and a few of them were large enough for a dozen or more.

Under the torches, I saw hooks with towels and robes waiting for bathers. As Bella had suggested, there was no one down here. No one except for Tristan and myself.

I turned to find Tristan and was surprised, though I shouldn't have been, to see that he had already removed his clothing. Shocked, I turned away from him. I'd seen him naked once before when he had greeted me at his bedroom door wearing nothing. I heard a splash and turned to see Tristan had selected one of the smaller pools. If I joined him in there, it was going to be very difficult to not bump into one another. I also knew that if I selected a different pool, he would either be insulted or join me anyway.

I silently cursed for not undressing before him and jumping in one of the larger pools to give me some more privacy or space. I'd given up the chance to control the situation. Hesitation was costing me and it was a good lesson to learn moving into Queen's Trial.

"Do you need me to close my eyes?" Tristan asked.

I could feel my cheeks heat. Thankfully, I was probably rather pink already from the temperature of the room which might hide my embarrassment. I played with the fabric on my sleeve as I considered what I should do. I still had time to run back up the stairs and find the privacy of my own room, but that was probably what Tristan wanted me to do. I was getting tired of his games and I had only just arrived here.

I didn't want to spend the next several weeks with him thinking he could control me by putting me in situations that made me uncomfortable. Then, I realized that the only one making me uncomfortable was me.

Fae didn't have the same sense of privacy that I had been raised with. I was the one who was giving him the power over me here when he might not even see nudity as an issue.

Before I could lose the nerve, I pulled my tunic over my head and covered my breasts with one arm. Then, I dropped my skirt to the floor in a puddle around my toes. I still had my underclothes on, and while they were sheer, they had enough fabric for me to feel like I was maintaining some sense of decorum. Even if it was a human trait, it was still so engraved in me that it felt like too much to be completely naked with Tristan.

I stepped over the fallen skirt, and walked to the small pool. Sitting down at the edge, I dipped a toe in, testing the warmth. It was warmer than I was used to for a bath, but not hot. Feeling braver, I dangled my legs into the water, relishing the sensation of the warmth. With a sigh, I slid into the pool. Water came up to my waist and I quickly ducked down so it covered my shoulders before releasing my arm from over my breasts. Now that I was in a small pool with Tristan, I wasn't sure what to do next.

He grinned at me, his icy blue eyes traveling from the water level up to my eyes. "That wasn't so hard, was it?"

"How did you know I was coming down here?" I asked. "Can you read my mind?"

Tristan shrugged. "On occasion, I see flashes from things inside your mind. But they don't seem to be things that have happened yet. Just things that might come to pass."

"Like what?" I asked, my pulse rising as I recalled the vision I had of the two of us entwined.

"Are you sure you want to know?" He moved a little closer. "I have to admit, the things that I've seen have been rather delicious."

I pursed my lips and bit back a snappy retort. He was bating me. The more time I spent with him, the more easily I was able to read him. He wanted me to get mad at him, but I didn't know why. I narrowed my eyes, trying to get a read on him and the pieces started to click into place. "You read Bella. Not me."

"Or maybe I just wanted to come down here," he said.

"You came down here for me," I said. "You sent me away, only to meet me here later. You push me away, then get closer to me. You flirt with me, but don't act on it."

"Have you stopped to think about the fact that maybe you're just as confusing to me?" He stood, water running down his sculpted chest and over his washboard abs. Tiny waves lapped around his hips, just barely covering his manhood.

I tore my eyes away from the waterline and looked up at his face. "I never hid anything from you. From the moment we met, I told you the truth."

"Have you, princess?" he asked, cocking his head to the side.

"Yes," I said. "I told you everything."

"You've kept nothing from me?" he asked.

My brow furrowed. What was he trying to get from me? Had I kept anything hidden away from Tristan? When we met, I didn't know about the magic I held or my ancestry. He'd been with me every step of the way while I learned about myself. "Nothing."

He let out a frustrated sigh. "Of course you haven't."

"What is that supposed to mean?" I asked.

"Nothing," he said, climbing out of the water. He stood on the edge of the pool, his wet body glistening in the warm, flickering torch light. "I'll send Bella for you. Stay as long as you like. You have a few more hours to rest, but I'll need your assistance tonight."

I leaned against the side of the pool. "Good. I'd like to get this over with so I can return to the Autumn Court."

He nodded, then turned and walked toward the wall and grabbed one of the robes off of a hook. He threw it over himself and walked out of the cave, not looking back at me.

Feeling equal parts irritated and anxious, I lowered myself into the water, holding my breath while I went under. Three weeks of Tristan's moods was going to be difficult to endure.

Chapter Nine

Below the water I felt like I had silence and peace the first time in weeks. There was something liberating about freeing yourself from your senses and existing below the surface. I held out as long as I could, slowly blowing bubbles out of my mouth to prolong the amount of time for a good stay under. Finally, my lungs started to protest, and I broke through to the surface, gasping for breath.

I moved my hair out of my face and wiped my eyes with the back of my hands. When I opened them, I saw Bella standing quietly with a robe draped over her arm.

I coughed a little, clearing some excess water and wiped my eyes again. "Have you been waiting long?"

"Only a moment. Did you want to stay longer? I can wait."

As much as I wanted to stay hidden underground and soak in the warm water, Tristan's words about needing me tonight rang through my mind. I didn't know what he had planned and it probably wouldn't hurt to try and get some rest while I had an opportunity to do so. I stood and walked over to the edge of the pool and pulled myself out. My undergarments clung to my skin, completely see-through from the water. Bella rushed over to me and wrapped the robe around me quickly tying the belt around the waist before I could offer to do it myself.

"What do you usually do around here?" I asked. If Tristan rarely had visitors, I wondered how often she was expected to wait on anyone aside from the Prince and anyone else who might live in the castle.

"I do whatever is required," Bella said.

I didn't press her, but I knew from her words she was hiding something. What could it be that she didn't want me to know? What kind of duties could Tristan ask of his servants that would cause her not to share with me? It seemed odd that there was something she left out after how freely she shared information before.

"As I said," Bella said, "we don't get a lot of visitors."

I nodded. "I can't imagine why. Tristan is just so charming." My words were sarcastic, but Bella didn't flinch.

"He can be, once you get to know him," Bella said.

I felt like I was getting to know Tristan pretty well. Which just meant I didn't know him at all. The more time I spent with him, the less sure I was about him. Before he brought me here, I had thought we were starting to connect on a personal level. And yet, here I was. Sucked into whatever his plan was, part of some greater master plan that he probably thought of the second he met me.

I wasn't sure what purpose I served, but at least I knew I had an end point. *Three weeks.* I wouldn't allow myself to consider the full five.

"Once we get upstairs I can do your hair, and you can rest a bit before the evening's festivities," Bella said.

"Festivities?" I asked as I followed Bella up the stairs.

"Of course, didn't his grace tell you?" Bella asked.

"I'm beginning to think he doesn't tell me anything." I frowned, thinking of how he had just questioned me. Of the two of us, I was the one who had been the most open. There wasn't anything I kept from him. It was possible, he even knew more about me than I knew about myself.

"There's a reception this evening. They didn't give me the details, but you're expected to be there," Bella said.

I didn't much feel like attending a party, but at least I knew Tristan would be distracted by his guests. Once I knew my way around better, maybe I could make an appearance and sneak out. It seemed an odd thing to have tonight considering the fact that Tristan had been traveling with me the last several days. How had he managed to plan it so quickly? Or was this on the agenda from the beginning? What if we had not made it to the Queen by now? Would he have just slid home and left the rest of us behind? Or had his plan all along been to bring me to this thing for some reason?

As we reached my door, exhaustion set in. I hadn't allowed myself to feel tired before, there were too many things to do and too much at stake. Now that I was looking at a bed, the only thing I wanted to do was get some sleep.

"Have a seat." Bella gestured to stool in front of the dressing table.

I obliged, letting my eyelids close for a moment and taking a few slow breaths. Bella didn't waste any time getting to work on my hair and I found myself getting more and more sleepy with each stroke of the brush. I felt pins touch my scalp and opened my eyes to look in the mirror.

Bella was carefully pinning my curls around my head in a trick I'd seen my human mother do on occasion. I knew this would allow me to sleep without my curls getting frizzy. Grateful that Bella was preparing me to rest, I watched as she finished. She hummed a tune as she walked across the room to the wardrobe pulled out some clothing and walked back. I recognize the song as something that Nani used to hum when I was a child. I wished she was here with me now. At least I knew she was alive and that I'd get to see her again soon.

"Try this," Bella said, holding up a nightgown.

Covering a yawn, I stood and let her help me into the clothes.

"I'll wake you when it's time to prepare. We still have a few hours and I'm sure you could use a nap," she said. "His Grace has assigned me to you for the tenure of your stay if it pleases you."

"Thank you, Bella," I said. "It will be nice to see a familiar face."

With a nod, she excused herself from the room, leaving me alone. I walked over to the window and checked to make sure it seemed like it was locked well enough to prevent any unwelcome visitors. Satisfied, I walked back to the bed and burrowed under the blankets. Now that I was alone in the near darkness, I felt hollow. I breathed in a clean, floral scent on the sheets. It made me feel even more alone. I missed the scent of the other princes. I missed feeling Dane's body against mine or Ethan's arms holding me close. I missed the taste of Cormac on my lips.

Tears slid down my cheeks and I allowed them to come as I pressed my face into the pillow. Three weeks. I was going to be here for at least three weeks. Cut off from the males who made me feel safe and comfortable. I was in a strange place with an unpredictable prince who had an agenda I couldn't figure out.

Quietly, I sobbed into the pillow, releasing all the pent up frustration and anger of the last week. It had been too long since I let myself go, unafraid of the consequences of someone seeing my tears. Finally, emotionally spent, I drifted into sleep.

I STOOD ALONE *in a burning field. Flames roared as they ate away at the landscape, sending pillars of black smoke rising into the air. Panic welled up inside me. Someone important had been right next to me, I'd been holding their hand, but now they were gone. I stretched my fingers out and tried to call out, but I wasn't sure which name I should cry for. Then, in the distance, I saw someone. A female in a gold dress. She wore a crown of fire and threw her head back in laughter. She turned to look at me and my blood ran cold as I found myself staring at Tiana. She smiled, perfectly happy to watch the world burn.*

I WOKE in a cold sweat and bolted up, sitting alone in the unfamiliar bed. It was dark in the room, but a small fire crackled merrily in the fireplace, offering an unstable light that made the room feel eerie. The light ebbed and flowed as the flames danced, casting ominous shadows that were gone as quickly as they appeared. My skin tingled in fear as I looked for anything that didn't look like it belonged.

I tossed the blankets aside and jumped from the bed, unsatisfied with my initial assessment. On tiptoes, I crept around the room, checking every corner. The only thing I found were shadows. Feeling relieved, but still on edge, I settled into one of the chairs near the fireplace and tried to calm my nerves. It hadn't even been a day in this place, and already I felt like I was losing touch with reality.

A gentle knock sounded on the door and I stood, then walked over to it. "Hello?"

The door opened and Bella peeked her head in. "My Lady, please tell me you slept."

"I did," I said. "I just woke. And please, call me Cassia."

She curtseyed. "Lady Cassia." She walked into the room and began to light the candles scattered around. She paused below a large chandelier in the center of the room and raised her hand toward it. The candles burst to life, a hundred flickering lights that illuminated the room as if it were daylight.

"How did you do that?" I asked.

She furrowed her brow. "Surely you learned how to light candles?"

I cleared my throat. "No. I'm actually quite behind in my magic studies."

"I can show you another time, but not tonight. Tonight, we

have to get you ready for the reception." Bella moved to the stool in front of the dressing table and waited for me to join her.

Reluctantly, I walked over to the table and sat on the stool. Learning magic sounded much more fun and much more useful than attending whatever formal event she was dressing me for.

As she pulled the pins out of my hair and went to work making me up for Tristan's reception, I thought back to my almost wedding day. The last time I'd put in effort to my appearance it hadn't paid off well for me. I hoped there were not going to be any monster attacks tonight. I smiled as I imagined how funny it might be to see a monster ruin Tristan's plans. I knew I shouldn't think that way, but he knew that I still didn't know how to contain my powers enough to prevent from attracting the creatures from the Under.

"You have beautiful hair," Bella said.

"Thank you," I said.

"You look a lot like your mother," she said.

I turned and looked at her. "You know who my mother is?"

"We all do," she said. "Tristan told the entire household while you slept. He's not exactly keeping it a secret. I would guess that if the entire Winter Court doesn't know about the two of you yet, they will by tomorrow."

"What do you mean by *the two of us*?" I asked.

"Your courtship, of course," she said. "Now that it's out in the open, you don't have to hide it from me anymore, my Lady. You have our full support. A lot of us have been waiting for a day like this. An alliance between Faerie and the Winter Court is a dream come true."

Chapter Ten

✦❖✦

"You can't be serious," I said. "Tristan and I are not courting."

She took her hand off of my hair and rested it on my shoulder. "It's alright, I know the official announcement isn't until tonight, but I've been keeping secrets for the Winter Prince for a long time. You can trust me."

"We are not courting," I repeated.

She chuckled softly and went back to working on my hair.

I clenched my teeth and took deep breaths as I stared at my reflection. My cheeks were bright red and the flush traveled down to my neck. Tristan was telling people we were courting? What purpose did that serve? How did that help anything?

Bella was humming again, happily ignoring my denials. She said she'd been assigned to me and that she'd been keeping Tristan's secrets for a long time. What did that mean, exactly? "Bella, how long have you worked for Tristan?"

"A long, long time, my Lady."

"What do you mean when you say you've been keeping his secrets?" I asked.

She shrugged. "I've served the royal family for nearly my

entire life. When you work as closely with them as I do, you're bound to learn things. And you gain their trust. Often, I am one of the first to know the news so I can help with transitions and changes as they occur."

"What exactly was your job before you were assigned to me?" I asked.

"I worked with His Grace on a special assignment," she smiled and ran her fingers through my hair, loosening the curls. "And now, he's having me work with you."

She was avoiding my questions so well she would have made Cormac proud. I suppose I wasn't privy to whatever she was hiding for Tristan yet. For some reason, knowing that Bella was part of Tristan's life through so many changes made me feel a little bit like I was being watched. And it also made me feel a little jealous. Which was completely unnecessary. I decided to change tactics. If she thought we were a couple, I needed to start asking the right kind of questions. "Tell me about the other females he's brought around."

"It's rare that he brings anyone here, my lady," she said.

"Has there been anyone since Lena?" I asked.

She stopped again, and took a step to the side so she could look at me better. "You know about Lena?"

"Yes." I had her attention. If I was going to get anything out of her, I had to push the relationship angle. "And I know how heartbroken he was. I don't want to see him go through that again. What can you tell me that I might need to know?"

Bella smiled, and returned to her position behind me. "He was heartbroken after she died. I'm sure you've heard the rumors about the parties and the females and the unnatural things happening in the Winter Court. But they were never about the Prince. He hasn't been the same since Lena died, that is true. But every rumor you've heard was likely about his brother. But nobody wants to hear that the little brother of the Heir is the villain. It's so much more exciting if it's about the Crown Prince."

"So it was never about him?" I asked. "Why didn't he stop the rumors? Or punish his brother?"

"He can't," she said. "There are things you don't know about him, but I can tell you, you should not doubt him. There's a reason I've chosen to work for him all this time. In a court full of evil and lies, the Prince gives me hope."

Bella's words weren't what I expected.

"Tristan sent a dress for you to wear," Bella said as she walked toward the wardrobe.

I stood, and followed her, wondering what was in store for me. I wasn't sure what to expect from Tristan. Especially now that I knew he was telling people that we were courting.

As soon as I got him alone, I was going to let him know exactly how I felt about him using me as a prop to play house with. I knew this was all connected to the real reason I was here and I had to admit, I was a little curious as to what he was planning. I'd give him a chance to explain before screaming at him. This would be a private conversation, but it needed to happen soon.

Bella held up a slim sparkling dress. Like all the other clothing Tristan had provided for me, it was in the colors of the Winter Court. Though this time, I noticed that the dress was far more silver than gray as it shimmered in the firelight. Bella held the dress for me so I could step into it carefully. Then she pulled it up over my hips and worked on fastening it up the back. I ran my hands along the curves of my body, all on display in the snug cut of the dress. Tiny black beads were sewn along the bodice, waist, and skirt in elegant patterns. Each tiny bead adding a flash of sparkle when the shiny surface caught the light. The fabric pooled at my feet, reminding me of a puddle of water as it shimmered. This was the kind of dress that only existed in stories. How was it that such a beautiful gown existed here? It was as if it had been made just for me. "It's stunning."

"Tristan's sister wore this dress to her coronation as Queen," Bella said.

My mouth felt dry as the weight of me wearing this dress sank in. I was a candidate for Queen's Trial and while Tristan hadn't spoken up to support me in front of my mother, he was going to show me off to his guests in a dress that belonged to a Queen. It was as if he already cast me into the role before the trial had even started.

Bella grabbed hold of my chin and turned it side to side.

I pulled away. "What are you doing?"

"Hold still." She opened one of the drawers in the dressing table and removed a few items. Then she added something to my lips quite a bit of kohl to line my eyes. Bella was nice, and I didn't want to give her a command, but I didn't like looking like someone who wasn't me. "Please, no more."

Bella nodded and returned the makeup drawer. "You really didn't need any at all. But it's a special night, sometimes it's nice to feel even prettier than usual."

I walked over to the mirror and looked at the very subtle makeup Bella had applied. It was tasteful and really did highlight my features rather than make me look different. My hair was half up, pinned with white flowers, while the rest of it flowed down my back. I couldn't help but smile at my reflection. Bella made me feel beautiful.

A knock sounded on the door and I jumped, my heart racing at the unexpected sound. Then, I realized it had to be Tristan to take me to his ridiculous reception and I was being jumpy for no reason. I wondered if I would get over the jitters I felt in response to every movement, shadow, and noise in the Winter Court. I wasn't comfortable here and I had a feeling that three weeks from now when I left, I still wouldn't feel at home.

Bella opened the door and dropped into a curtsy. "Your grace."

I walked to the door, my dress a swish of fabric as I moved.

I froze when I saw Tristan. He'd cleaned up just as much as I had and tonight, he looked every bit the Prince he was supposed to be. If he wanted people to think we were a couple, the clothing choices would aid in the illusion. We were a matched set in silver and black.

Tristan inclined his head and offered his hand. "My Lady."

I was still stunned by his appearance, struggling to tear my gaze away from him. His silver tunic was cut to show his lean form, rounded shoulders and firm biceps visible under the silky fabric. Fitted trousers completed the ensemble, reminding me just how powerful his legs had looked without his clothes on. For a second, I lingered on the bulge where his manhood was. I knew he was well endowed and it was obvious in the snug fit of his clothes tonight.

He cleared his throat and I looked up at him, biting down on my lip in embarrassment. "You look..." I stumbled for the words, trying to come up with a compliment that didn't convey the fact that heat was rising low in my belly sending treacherous shivers of desire between my legs. "Very handsome."

His blue eyes sparkled and he brushed a few falling strands of his blond hair away from his eyes before lifting his offered hand. The grin on his face looked like genuine happiness. "You look even more stunning than I could've imagined."

"Thank you," I said. Either the years of being forced to use proper manners were overtaking any anger at him or I was too lost in his changed appearance. It wasn't that he wasn't usually handsome. He was gorgeous even covered in dirt and blood. There was something about him cleaned up and trying to impress me that made me look at him differently. Or was it Bella's comments about him that were getting to me? Either way, I felt like I was seeing him for the first time.

I took a breath and tried not to think about how handsome he looked. "You and I need to have a conversation."

"I agree. But it will have to wait. Our guests are waiting."

Frustrated, I folded my arms over my chest. "We really need

to talk." Did he understand I was trying to give him an opportunity to talk in private?

"I know, but we let you sleep in. The party started an hour ago. People are starting to talk," he said.

"They shouldn't be talking about me at all," I said reluctantly moving toward him.

"You can't expect me to hide away a gem like you." He winked.

I wanted to be mad, but I couldn't hold on to the anger. Reluctantly, I set my hand in his. "Except you're forgetting, Your Grace, I don't belong to you."

"I would never forget that. You don't belong to anyone. That's one of the few things you and I agree on," he said, pulling me closer to him. "As I told you when we met, I fully anticipate that one day you'll come to me. Until then, you're my guest, only here until your favor is fulfilled."

"I don't recall anything about my favor involving showing me off to people I've never met," I said.

"Oh, I promise you, it directly relates," Tristan said as led me down the hall and down the stairs.

I took a deep breath as the sound of laughter, clinking glasses, and music grew louder with each step. There really was a party going on. I wasn't in the mood for a party. Curiosity seemed to guide me, though. How had Tristan connected a party to his desire to learn about human customs?

"You could at least pretend you're enjoying my company," Tristan said.

"Is that part of the bargain?" I asked.

"No," he admitted. "But if you let your guard down, you might accidentally have some fun."

A slight smile found its way across my lips. I *was* stuck here, after all. And I had fun at the Fae wedding I'd stumbled across even after all my doubts. "Alright. I'll try."

We paused outside of a pair of double doors that were open wide, revealing a ballroom packed to the brim. Most of the guests were wearing the colors of the Winter Court. I wondered if that was the trend of the Winter Court of if they were all part of Tristan's family. I squeezed Tristan's hand tight, suddenly feeling nervous.

I glanced around the room, looking for a place I could go to be out of the way. Several figures were standing off to the side, avoiding most of the other guests, engaged in conversation.

They were different than the rest of the guests, smaller in stature, their skin had none of the iridescent quality that I'd come to know as a Fae quality. The group of humans stood out more than I thought they would. How had I never noticed how small and frail humans looked before?

Tristan leaned down next to me, his lips brushed against my ears. "I see you found the humans. Now you see why I need your assistance."

I looked up at Tristan. "I thought humans weren't allowed in this realm."

"They aren't allowed in Faerie. But we're not *in* Faerie." Tristan slid his arm under mine so we were linking elbows. "Come, let me introduce you."

Following Tristan's lead, we cut through the crowd easily. Heads lowered in reverence as we passed and partygoers backed out of our way with whispers of, "*Your Grace.*"

I felt like thousands of eyes were on me and I was suddenly self-conscious of every move I made. Knots twisted in my gut and I could hear my pulse pounding in my ears over the din of the crowd. Everyone wanted a glimpse of the Winter Prince, which meant all eyes were also on me.

I moved in closer to Tristan, using my free hand to wrap my fingers around his firm bicep to make sure I didn't lose him. Knowing the strength and power of the Fae and being in a room of this many made me incredibly uncomfortable, even if I was one of them. I still didn't feel totally safe but having Tristan by my side helped.

There was something different about this crowd from the crowd that had gathered for the wedding I attended. Everyone here was clearly of noble birth, or somehow had risen to the highest classes in this society.

The wedding had been simple. Everyone there had turned out in their best, but it was to celebrate the love between the couple who was getting married. This was a peacock parade. The guests here were showing off their finery, and vying for power and position. It was exactly the same as the parties I'd attended with my father. Tristan said he wanted my help with the humans, but from what I was seeing, there was nothing different between the way the Fae acted and the way humans acted when it came to things like this.

We stopped in front of the small group of humans, all men, all dressed in the highest quality fabrics. They ranged in age. The youngest looking to be in his early twenties while the eldest, a completely white haired man, was probably closer to sixty. Every one of them bowed at Tristan and greeted him with a chorus of, "*Your Grace*," then then turned to me and bowed, bestowing the same title on me. I felt my cheeks heat at the group of men calling me, "*Your Grace.*"

I glanced at Tristan, looking for guidance as to how I should react. Tristan didn't even flinch at their use of the title on me. I still had no idea what he wanted from me, but he didn't seem to care if they had my station correct.

"How are you adjusting to life in the Fae Court after all your time in the human realm?" the youngest member of the group asked.

I blinked in surprise, staring at him with unease. I'd been told to keep my history as a changeling secret and there was no way I'd pass as human anymore. I knew my skin and my ears would give me away to these men.

"It's fine," I said, choosing what I hoped was a vague and diplomatic answer.

"You were likely just as surprised to find out you were Fae as we were to get an invitation to the Winter Court," a dark haired man said.

"I'm sure," I said.

"I would love to hear your thoughts on the human-Fae alliance. You must have the most balanced understanding of both cultures," the youngest man said.

"I'm not sure yet," I said. "I haven't had time to fully process it all." What was Tristan's purpose in bringing these men here and what did he want from me? Obviously, his human question was more important than I realized. I never guessed he was interacting with humans. But it still didn't make any sense. The room seemed to spin around me. I wasn't prepared for any of this.

Needing a moment to collect myself, I inclined my head and bobbed into a tiny curtsey. "Gentlemen, if you'll excuse me, I need to get some air."

"Of course, Your Grace," the youngest man said, bowing.

The others bowed as I turned away from them to take my leave. To my surprise, Tristan didn't follow. I wondered how much time he'd give me before he came to collect me again.

Chapter Eleven

Mumbled conversation and whispers followed in my wake as I made my way through the crowd back to the double doors. Unable to focus, the figures around me blurred together into a sea of gray and black satin and silk.

I hadn't expected to be part of the social calendar of the Winter Court when I had followed Tristan here. Not that he'd given me a choice, but he could've given me fair warning.

I started to wonder if it would be worth breaking the favor and giving up all of my magic. I hadn't even wanted it in the first place. So far, it had caused me nothing but trouble. It attracted monsters, and it put a target on my back. If I went back to the Autumn Court, Tristan could just have my magic. I could explain that I wasn't eligible or interested in participating in Queen's Trial and maybe I could just learn a trade and live in a small village somewhere.

My stomach clenched. Even as I thought about it, I knew it wasn't possible. The magic was part of me whether or not I knew how to use it. I had a feeling if I eliminated it, I would have to pay too high a price. I wandered down the hallways not really thinking about where I was going, turning down one hall into another, letting myself get lost.

Tristan hadn't forbidden me from going anywhere, he probably thought I wouldn't even bother to try, so I just kept wandering while I let my breathing return to normal. I wasn't good around crowds, I never had been. How was I going to make it in Queen's Trial if I was going to be expected to do things like this? Mingling with nobles and diplomats and smiling and nodding were not things that sounded fun. I'd avoided it whenever possible in the human realm and until the Sodalis attack, nobody had been trying to kill me there.

I heard voices behind me and panic welled up inside me. I wasn't ready to go back yet. I would in a few minutes, I needed a little more time. Without thinking, I opened the nearest door and ducked inside whatever the room was, closing the door quietly behind me. I leaned against the wood and closed my eyes, taking deep breaths while I listened for any sound outside the door.

Satisfied that no one had seen me, I open my eyes and stared into a dimly lit room. It looked to be a small parlor of some sort, with a few places to sit and a few small tables for games or other diversions. A light appeared in the corner and I turned toward it letting out a startled gasp when I realized I wasn't alone. In an overstuffed armchair sat a thin, frail looking female. She had stringy, long golden hair and her dress hung from her thin frame, showing her visible collar bones and the upper bones of her ribs. Her eyes were sunken and she had a hollow, sad expression.

"I'm so sorry to have disturbed you," I said. "I'll be on my way."

"Wait," the female said. "I recognize that dress."

My hand was already on the doorknob, but I let go of it and turned back to her. There was something about her voice that seemed familiar. But I couldn't place it. "Tristan lent it to me."

"So you're the one they've been talking about," she said. "I wondered if my brother was ever going to introduce us."

Tristan's memory flashed into my head, a young boy in the protective embrace of his older sister. "Sasha?" I asked.

She smirked, making her look even more like Tristan. "So he has shared his magic with you, that's very interesting."

"I don't know what you're talking about," I said quickly. Tristan had trusted me with his ability to share memories and while I might not be happy with him right now, I had made a promise never to share that information. In the list of people who knew what he could do, Sasha had not been among them.

"And you're protective of him too," she said. "I can see why he likes you. You know," Sasha said. "I had my doubts when I heard the rumblings about you. But now I'm starting to think my brother knows what he's doing."

"I don't even know what your brother's doing," I said.

"Maybe it's time for you to have a little bit of faith in others. Even if someone let you down in the past, sometimes there are very good reasons people do the things they do." Sasha picked up a little bell and gave it a shake. It jingled with a sharp chime.

The door opened almost immediately and Bella walked in. "Yes, my Lady?"

"Bella?" I asked. "Is this your position here?"

She turned to me. "Lady Cassia." She looked at Sasha.

"Yes, Bella has helped care for me for a long time. She's the only servant in the house who knows how to help care for a female. When my brother let me know you'd be staying with us, I demanded he send her to you until Tristan could find you proper help. I can't imagine anyone else trying to prepare you for a party."

"I didn't mean to take her from you," I said. "I can manage fine on my own."

"I don't mind sharing," Sasha said. "But I do need to rest.

Bella, can you please fetch a guard to escort Lady Cassia back to the party?"

"Of course, my Lady," Bella said with a curtsy. She ducked out the door.

Before I could ask any more questions, a guard appeared at the door. He lowered his head in a reverent bow. "My Lady."

"Please escort our guest back to the party," Sasha said with a tiny wave of her hand.

He bowed again. "Of course."

"It was lovely to meet you," I said.

Sasha nodded, then waved her hand at me, dismissing me.

I was curious about Sasha's history and wondered why she was sitting in here alone while the party was going on down the hall. Nothing turned out to be as it seemed in the Winter Court. With one final glance at Sasha, I decided she wasn't going to give me any information. I walked toward the guard at the door, and waited while he shut the door behind us.

"This way, my Lady," the guard said. He was formal and stiff as we walked down hall, taking his order from Sasha very seriously without any additional comment. His body language made it clear that he wasn't interested in having a conversation with me. All too soon, I found myself facing the doors that lead to the celebration.

I'd left so abruptly, I was dreading Tristan's reaction to my return. With a deep breath, I imagined myself marching right up to him demanding answers. Keeping that in mind, I lifted my chin high and crossed the threshold.

When I walked into the party, no one was mingling anymore. Instead, music filled the space and the room was a swirl of fabric and movement as the elegant attendees made their way across the dance floor.

Hugging the wall, I worked my way into the room, searching for Tristan. It didn't take me long to find him, wrapped up with a female I didn't know, laughing, cheeks pink from exertion. Tristan and his guest moved with ease and grace around the dance floor. The female in his arms wore a deep blue dress that swirled around her with every turn and spin. Gems woven into her midnight black hair winked and sparkled, creating the illusion of a crown on top of her head. She threw her head back as she laughed, batting long dark lashes. If there was a female in this room that was my opposite in appearance, she was it. She was stunning and I felt the uncomfortable stab of jealousy in my gut. My cheeks heated despite the fact that I told myself that I had no interest in Tristan.

I had three princes waiting for me, each of whom had pledged themselves to me. Why should I care what or whom the Winter Prince did in his own time?

Clearly, he didn't care about me. I was here to fulfill some strange part of his master plan that had nothing to do with the rest of Faerie. I leaned against the wall, fuming as I watched Tristan continue to flit around the dance floor with the stranger.

My fingernails bit into my palms as I clenched my hands into fists. It was possible he didn't even miss me while I was gone. I stared at him, willing him to look my way. I wanted him to see how angry I was after more half-truths from the sister he kept hidden from me. But he was fixated on his partner, his gaze never wavered.

The longer I stood there, the more heat seemed to ride through me sending a surge of jealousy that I couldn't subdue. I glanced back toward the door and wondered if I should just take off again. I could probably find my way back to the room where they dressed me up for this spectacle.

"Glad to see you came back," a male voice said. I turned to see the youngest of the group of humans leaning against the wall next to me. He was a couple of inches taller than me with dark hair and dark stubble. Circles under his eyes told me he hadn't been sleeping well lately. I suddenly felt sorry for him. Faerie was very different from the human world and while I'd had time to adjust and I knew this was where I belonged, he was even more out of place than I was.

"How long have you been here?" I asked.

"In the Winter Court?" he asked.

I nodded. "Significant change from the human realm."

"That is very true." He smiled and seemed to relax a little as we spoke. "We've been coming back and forth for short visits for a few months now. This will be the first time we stay overnight."

"And you've just been working with Tristan?" I asked.

"Yes, the prince reached out to us, looking for an opportunity to open up trade routes and diplomatic discussions between our realm and yours."

I thought about his words, and the fact that he came from the place I used to think of as home. Now, I supposed this realm was home. As much as I felt like I belonged here, I still had moments where it seemed surreal and impossible. "Are you a prince?"

"No." He laughed. "I do represent one, though." He extended his hand. "I'm Jonathan Rivers, Ambassador for the Kingdom of Marta. I've been helping to work on negotiating a treaty on his behalf."

I shook the man's hand, surprised that he offered me the gesture. I was used to women being ignored in terms of formal introduction. "And this is something you all want? Diplomatic relations and trade between the Fae and the humans?"

"I'm sure it would make things easier for you," he said. "I can't imagine being in your position, trapped between two worlds."

His comment surprised me and I wondered how much of my story he knew. I realized I had two options. One, I could pretend that I knew what Tristan's plans were. Two, I could ask questions and possibly get answers since this man didn't seem to think there was any reason to hide anything from me.

I knew I needed to be smart about it. Letting him know that Tristan was keeping me in the dark might make him stop discussing things with me. "How much of my past have you already been told?" I figured sticking to things that were about me might be the safest route to feel him out.

"Oh don't worry," he said. "His Grace explained the situation to us. How you were left behind when your family was visiting the human realm, sole survivor of a gruesome attack. It's tragic that anyone could be so unaccepting of those who were different. We're grateful that he was able to rescue you."

I bit down inside of my cheek to keep from laughing. Apparently, Tristan had painted himself the hero in my tragic story. I wondered what purpose this was serving for him.

The music faded as the song ended and out of the corner of my eye, I saw the crowd disperse from the dance floor. I turned away from Jonathan instinctively searching for Tristan.

"You know," Jonathan said as I continued to scour the crowd. "I don't think I've ever heard a more epic love story between two people."

I glanced over at Jonathan, confused for a moment before remembering that Tristan was telling everyone we were a couple. I smiled slightly and turned my attention back to the crowd. This time, I wasn't going to allow Tristan to get away with not having a discussion with me. This had gone far enough.

Finally, among the crowd, I found Tristan bowing to his dance partner. He still hadn't seemed to notice I was waiting for him. I scowled, knowing that it was all probably part of some part of his plan. Tristan always seemed to know where I was and what I was doing. How often had he shown up when I didn't want him to? How often had he interrupted me with others for his own entertainment? Tristan had to know I was here, which meant he was ignoring me.

I turned to Jonathan. "Excuse me."

I didn't wait for any sort of response or comment back from the human male before heading out into the crowd. When I approached Tristan, he was laughing and chatting animatedly with the female he had shared the dance with. I stopped next to the two of them, waiting for him to turn toward me.

Finally, Tristan tore his eyes away from the other female and looked over at me, a grin on his face. "Cassia, glad you returned. I'd like you to meet Lady Anya, my youngest sister."

I bit down on my lip as I repressed letting out a sigh of relief. The female he'd been so fixated on was another sister. She didn't look anything like Tristan, but I knew that his father had bedded multiple females in an attempt to gain offspring that were more powerful. I wondered where she hailed from and what her mother looked like. She was stunning, a dark-haired beauty who looked out of place among the silver and pale tones of the Winter quarter. Her dark blue dress and the sparkling jewels in her hair, set her apart from the rest of the guests.

Anya dipped her chin. "Lovely to meet you, Cassia. I've heard so much about you."

I wondered when Tristan had time to tell everyone about me. We only met a few days ago. Had he spent the few hours I was sleeping catching everyone up on my life story? I forced a smile on my lips. "It's nice to meet you."

I glanced at Tristan and then looked back at Anya. "I hate to do this, but can I steal him for a few moments?"

Anya dipped her head again. "Of course. Take all the time you need."

I grabbed Tristan's hand and tugged him after me before he could have time to object. He interlaced his fingers with mine, and I was surprised to find his touch comforting. I resisted the first few times I had physical contact with him, but now feeling his large hand wrapped around mine gave me a sense of security that I knew I shouldn't believe. Nothing around Tristan was as it seemed. Even if he never lied to me, he had a way of distorting the truth that was nearly the same thing.

"You're in such a hurry. Others might get the wrong idea about us," Tristan said.

I glanced back at him then returned my attention ahead of us. I cut through the crowd toward the doors. "What idea might that be?"

"Well, I do have a reputation of sneaking off during events like this with beautiful females. I'm sure they'll come to their own conclusions about what the two of us are doing in such a rush," Tristan said.

If he was trying to get me to return to the party and avoid having this conversation because he thought I was worried about my reputation, he had another thing coming. As far as either of us knew, my reputation was already ruined. And hadn't everyone been telling me that sex wasn't a big deal here?

I held his hand tighter, worried he was going to break free before we got to the doors. "Let them think what they want. Or I'm going to start telling them things you might not want them to know."

The guard at the door stepped aside for us as he straightened to attention for Tristan. Once we were in the hall, I turned toward the Prince. "We need to talk. You need to start explaining things to me. If I'm stuck here, I need to know what's going on. I don't appreciate you telling everyone we're engaged and the only reason I haven't said anything is because I know you protected me. I just don't know what game you're playing anymore. I thought I knew who you were, but I was wrong."

"You're right, you don't know who I am at all."

Chapter Twelve

"Enough, Tristan," I said. "I'm tired of the games. No more pretending to be something terrible. You're not as bad as you want me to think you are. I can see right through you."

"What makes you think you know me at all?" he said.

"I know you'd never hurt me. And I know you don't like it when people use you for their own gain. So how about you start trusting me a little bit and letting me in? You might be surprised at how I react."

He was quiet, staring at me unblinking.

I thought about my whirlwind day in the Winter Court. He'd brought me here to help him with humans, but there was no reason for him to tell people we were a couple. Something else was going on, which I'd long suspected, but I didn't know what it could be.

"Why do you care what my plans are for you? You can smile and play along, and help me understand these humans. When your time's up, simply tell them the arrangements no longer fit our needs and you can leave."

My mouth dropped open as a pang of disappointment shot through me. "What is wrong with you? Why can't you just be honest with me? If you dislike having me around so much, why drag me here and go through all of this? You don't need me."

"That's where you're wrong," he said. "Those humans will trust me because of you."

"They won't if I don't play along. You took a huge gamble on this. How did you know I wouldn't just out you to them right away? There's nothing in our bargain about me pretending to be your lover."

"For once, can you just trust me? I know you don't want to be here. I promise I will never hurt you. I need you to go with this."

"But you have deceived me, you've tricked me, you've hidden things from me. Has it ever occurred to you that maybe I would be willing to help you if you just told me what it was I was helping with?"

Tristan opened his mouth as if he was going to say something, then closed it. He shook his head.

I took a deep breath and raised my eyebrows, silently encouraging him to explain.

"That's not how things work around here. You don't understand. We aren't in the Autumn Court. Anything you know, anything that's in your head, it's fair game for the taking. You're in the Winter Court now. A court of mind readers and people who can see the future. The less you know, the safer you are."

I tensed, struggling to find a way to argue against these words. He had a point I hadn't considered. Whatever he had up his sleeve was in his head alone and anyone who wanted to know what he was planning simply had to look inside his head to find all the answers. "What about you?"

"There are ways to protect yourself, things you can learn over time. You're not ready for that yet. It takes years of practice."

"And all of this - whatever you're having me play out has something to do with the favor you asked of me?" I asked.

"I meant what I said. I need your help with the humans. I need them on my side and I need them to trust me. I know the only way I'm going to get what I want is if I have you by my side."

My brow furrowed. "So you can see my future."

"Can you just trust me on this? I'm begging you, Cassia." Tristan lifted his hand and moved to touch my cheek I held my breath in anticipation of the touch, but it never came. Instead, he lowered his hand and I watched as he pulled his fingers into a fist.

"The first trial will arrive any day. Soon as you solve that, they'll send the next one. When all three are done, you will be free to go. In the meantime, I could use your help with this. I should've asked, but I didn't know you then. I made a poor call, but it is in both our best interests. I promise you, everything I've done has been with thoughts of your safety in mind."

"You've gotta give me something, Tristan. You haven't earned my trust enough for me to follow you blindly."

Tristan tightened his jaw, then he swallowed. "I deserve that. And you're right. You know how the human world is, they don't listen to females the way we do here. Bringing you in as my betrothed gives you a status that they could understand. It was last-minute, something I realized when I overheard them speaking."

"You seem to understand human politics very well on your own," I said. "What can I possibly teach you about them?"

"Mannerisms, things they say, body language, subtleties." He reached for me again, this time taking my hand in his. "Our cultures are different and I pride myself on being able to read Fae, but so much of that comes from being able to see into their minds and their futures. I can't read human minds. I'm going to need your help on that."

"I can't read their minds," I said.

"No, but you're perceptive and your intuition will serve you well here. Please, I can't tell you anymore yet."

I closed my eyes and took a deep breath, frustrated at how badly I wanted to help Tristan. I wanted to find resistance to helping him. I wanted something in my intuition to flare and send a warning, but there was nothing. There was no reason I could find to turn him down. In fact, it was quite the opposite. I wanted to help him and I found that I wanted to spend more time with him, which made me feel like I was betraying my own thoughts and my heart. But I knew I had to follow my instincts and I wasn't sure I'd even have a choice, anyway.

Despite his mood swings, Tristan had never hurt me and it was possible he was protecting me in the only way he knew how. I opened my eyes and looked into the icy blue gaze staring down at me. He was patient, studying my features with a relaxed expression, as if giving me all the time in the world.

"I'll help you, but you're going to have to start trusting me. You can't keep me in the dark forever."

Tristan was silent, the muscles in his temple jumping as he tightened his jaw.

"Give me something. Anything. Don't close me out." I gently set my fingers on his upper arm.

Of all four princes, Tristan had started out the most open and willing to share the truth. The closer we got, the more he seemed to shut down. He reminded me in some ways of Cormac, who closed himself off from me anytime I started to break the surface of his hurt. Only now, Cormac was moving in the opposite direction, finally starting to open up to me.

Tristan glanced around, as if checking to make sure we were still alone. "You recall the assassin?"

I nodded, how could I forget?

"And you know she was sent for me, not you." He licked his lips, pausing. It was as if whatever he wanted to get out was painful or difficult to say.

I waited patiently, keeping my hand pressed against his arm.

"My father sent that assassin. Things are in motion that will mean a lot of turmoil in the Winter Court. A war is brewing. I'm sorry I had to involve you. I promise it is safer for you this way."

I dropped my hands, unable to find the words to respond to his admission. I knew his father was a tyrant. I also knew he had children with as many different females as he could and had them all tested in the hopes that some of them might have more power. Even with all that, even after going through my own father trying to sell me off, I didn't expect to hear that the Winter King would try to have his son and heir killed. "I thought you had taken over for your father."

"Not because he stepped down. Only because he quit showing up and our court was on the verge of collapse. Someone had to and my siblings asked me to step up. Apparently, he's now viewing that as a threat against his own throne."

"Your Grace?" a guard called out as he approached us.

Tristan turned away from me to face the guard. "What is it?"

"You told me to let you know if your human guests left the party. They seem to be losing interest."

Tristan shook his head then turned back to me. "I need your help. How do I get them on my side?"

"This isn't about trade, is it?" I asked, already knowing the answer. It all rushed into me at once, flashes of thoughts, short bursts of emotions that didn't belong to me. Anger and frustration and sadness twisted together and I suddenly knew what Tristan was after.

My eyes widened as recognition crept in and I knew what Tristan was planning. All of it. Everything he had in mind flooded into me in an instant as if he'd poured his entire plan into me. I wouldn't be able to explain it all if I tried, but I could feel it. Suddenly, I knew what this was really about. Tristan was going to make a play against his father to take control of the Winter Court. But his father had already convinced the noble houses to support him so Tristan needed reinforcements. That's where the humans came in.

"Thank you, Henry." Tristan waved his hand dismissing the guard.

As the guard walked away, I caught Tristan's hand. "I understand what you're doing. And I'll help."

"All I need you to do is get those humans on my side," Tristan said. "I don't want you involved in any of the other parts of this."

"I'll do my best," I said. Then I walked back down the hall toward the ballroom, straightening my shoulders as I approached the doors. Lifting my chin, I walked through the room carrying myself as I expected a future Queen might. Casually, I walked over to where the humans were standing and I could tell from their hunched shoulders and darting eyes that they were intimidated by the others in this room. Humans were taught to fear magic, it was viewed as evil and punished without mercy. I needed to show them the truth and beauty of what magic could accomplish and that it wasn't something to be feared.

As I approached, I noticed that some of them seemed to relax around me. Being female, I was probably seen as less of a threat. Add in the fact that I understood what their life was like and had been raised as a human myself, meant they could relate to me.

I smiled as I stopped in front of the group and inclined my head in greeting. "I apologize for my abrupt departure. I'm still not comfortable in gatherings like this. I know I'm not human, but I still feel human. While I know none of them will hurt me, being around so many Fae can be overwhelming."

I tried to give what I hoped was a knowing expression, as if we shared a secret. "But I don't need to explain that to all of you, do I? I should have asked you gentlemen if you also needed some air."

The oldest member of the group chuckled and a couple others smiled at me. Tristan was right, they were more relaxed and at ease with me than they were with him. But if I was going to help him, I needed to build their trust enough that they could direct that trust to Tristan. Reminding myself that by helping him I was saving his life and helping the Fae who called the Winter Court home, I slipped into the role of fiancée and future Princess. "I'm incredibly grateful for the patience His Grace has had with me. I ask a lot of foolish questions, but he always indulges me. And so have his friends. The Fae really are nothing like the horror stories we were raised with in the human realm."

The oldest member of the group leaned forward a bit, clearly intrigued by my words. I had his attention, now I needed to keep it.

"Did you know that they have healing powers? They can help relieve injury and treat those that need repaired. And there are Fae who help things grow or who understand animals. It's a rather whimsical world, full of beauty unlike anything I ever saw in the human realm. Can you imagine what life might be like if we didn't have to worry about crops growing or watching our loved ones die of fever?"

"Surely, you miss your childhood home," Johnathan said.

"Of course I miss aspects of my human life." I swallowed a lump in my throat, surprised at my very real feelings emerging. "But surely, you realize how much better things are for me here? If we were in the human world, you wouldn't even be speaking to me. I'd have no power and no authority. Here, I can promise you that whatever I say will hold as much weight as that of any man."

The oldest man smirked and extended his hand. "I'm Clive, we haven't been formally introduced."

I extended my hand and shook in the simple human gesture. As I did, I felt powerful and comfortable in the role I'd stepped into. I could almost feel Tristan's approval even though he wasn't standing here with me. He wanted me to play the role of his future Queen, and I decided I'd go all in. Any female who was going to be able to handle a life with the stubborn prince would need to have nerves of steel and she'd need to be just as sure of herself as he was. For the sake of appearances, I'd stepped into that role.

"Clive, gentlemen," I nodded to the group, "please think of me as your translator between the realms. While I'm still learning about the nuances of the Faerie ways, I will do my best to navigate you through the process of becoming our allies. As someone who has lived on both sides, I can tell you, life is inherently better with magic."

An arm wrapped around my shoulders and I tensed, ready to pull away. Then, Tristan's lips touched my cheeks. "I see you've returned to the party, princess. Welcome back. I trust you're feeling refreshed?"

I smiled at him, continuing the act, as very real warmth spread through my whole body from his touch. "I am, thank you."

"Where we come from, women would never be interested in discussions of politics or alliances," one of the older men said.

I narrowed my eyes at him. "Where you come from, you don't allow women a chance. Perhaps if you took some time to have actual conversations you might realize they have something to offer."

"Our traditions are different here," Tristan offered. "We have long been ruled by Queens. Until the Winter Court broke from the rest of Faerie. Here in our realm, we have a king."

"A partnership, you mean," I said.

"Very true, I'd never ignore her advice or suggestions," Tristan pulled me closer to him.

"The point is, that investing with us is an investment in the future. Your realm is set in old ways that have long held you back," I said.

"If we help you," Clive said, "and you gain the throne. Then what becomes of our alliance?"

"It thrives," I said. "And you know Fae can't tell a lie."

Chapter Thirteen

❧❦❧

"You were amazing," Tristan said as we stood in front of my bedroom door. "Now you see why I needed you and your knowledge of humans here."

"I do," I said. "However, it doesn't excuse the secrets and hidden agendas. How do you know I wouldn't have just agreed to help if you'd asked?"

"You wouldn't have, that much I know," he said.

I pursed my lips. It was difficult to argue with someone who could see the future. It was possible he had looked into my response. "Not because I didn't want to help you, I can assure you. It's just not great timing for me. I have Queen's Trial to think about. Plus..." my thoughts drifted to the princes I'd left behind.

"I'm sure they're all pining away for you right now," he said, his expression hardening. "Good night."

"Tristan, don't do that," I said.

"Do what?" he asked.

"Shut me out because I'm in love with someone who isn't you. You're the one who brought me here."

He chuckled. "You think I'm jealous?"

"Aren't you?" I asked.

He shook his head. "No, princess. They can have you."

My shoulders fell and a weight settled into the pit of my stomach. I'd been telling myself I had no interest in Tristan yet hearing him say those words shattered something inside me. I lifted my chin, feigning nonchalance as best I could.

I turned the handle of the door. "Good night, Tristan."

"Good night, princess," he said, turning away from me.

I lingered in front of the open door, watching him as he walked away. He never turned to look at me. Maybe he really wasn't jealous. Maybe he really didn't care about me. Not that I should care. Tristan wasn't good for me and I knew that. Why was it so hard for me to ignore him?

Feeling more confused than usual, I stepped into the room to find a familiar face waiting for me in the corner of the room. All thoughts of Tristan vanished as I squealed and ran toward Nani.

My old maid returned my eager embrace, the two of us holding on longer than necessary. It was as if she knew that I was afraid to let her go. Finally, I broke the embrace and stepped back to look at her. "You're here. Thank the gods you're alive."

Nani smiled. "Hush now, child. No reason to be so worked up. I'm here now and I'm not leaving you again."

"How are you here?" I asked.

Her brow furrowed. "I thought you sent for me?"

My eyes widened. "No, not that I didn't want you here, I just never knew I could."

"Don't worry, child," she said. "His Grace must have known you needed some company."

"His Grace - you mean Ethan or Cormac or Dane, right?" I asked.

"The Winter Prince," she said. "He sent word to the Queen that you were in need of a maid and thought you would benefit from a familiar face. He asked her to send you some company."

"Tristan sent for you?" I asked.

"Yes, he did," she said.

"What happened after my father took you away? How did you escape? Why didn't you tell me who I really was?" The questions poured out of me at rapid fire pace.

"All in good time," she said. "I will answer all of your questions, but not right now. You need rest. You've been through quite the ordeal."

I couldn't deny that and once the words left her mouth, I realized how tired I was. I did need rest. "Tomorrow."

"Tomorrow," she agreed.

❦

I WOKE to the smell of something sweet and familiar, like the breakfast cakes I'd had on holidays as a child. My nose twitched and I squeezed my eyes shut harder, trying to decide if the smell was real. The sound of someone moving around the room forced me to open my eyes.

Sunlight poured in through the sheer curtains and I squinted against the surprisingly bright light. I hadn't seen sunshine that intense since coming to the Winter Court. As I adjusted to the light, I relaxed my grip on the bedding I'd been squeezing in my grasp. It was Nani moving around the room, humming gently as she set out plates and food on the small table in front of the windows.

I tossed back the blankets and padded over to her, careful not to disturb her routine. She looked happy and at ease as she moved things from a cart to the table. I glanced behind me to see that the bedroom door was still closed. How had she managed to get the cart and food in here without waking me?

"Good morning," Nani said without looking up at me.

"Good morning," I said, padding over to the small table near the window. The cold floor stung my bare feet but I ignored it, too eager to sit with Nani.

She pulled out a chair for me and inclined her head toward the waiting seat. Without a word I sat and waited as she took the chair opposite mine. She set sweet cakes on my plate, then propped her chin up with her hands as she had done when I was a child. How many mornings had she sat and listened to me talk while she watched me eat?

I set down the cake that was in my hand, my stomach twisting in guilt. In all that time, I'd never once asked her to eat with me. I'd thought myself kind and welcoming because she sat at the table with me, but I'd never once offered for her to join me.

I pushed the plate the extra cakes were on toward her and divided the food between the two of us. "Eat, please."

"I made them for you, child," she said.

"Please, don't make me have breakfast alone," I said.

She smiled and lifted a cake. "Only because we're in the Winter Court. Once we return, I'll have to abide by the rules of the Autumn Court."

"Why?" I asked.

"There is much you have to learn about the way things are done in Faerie," she said.

"Like the fact that I was hidden away?" I asked. "Nani, everything is so different here."

She set the cake down on her plate. "It is different, but you are not ill prepared. You grew up in a household where power was mistaken for wealth and wealth was an illusion. How you dressed, who you knew, and who you married your children to was how a man measured his worth. The Fae Courts aren't much different. They all claim to be above such human pettiness, but they aren't. Believe it or not, the things you witnessed growing up are going to benefit you in Queen's Trial more than you think."

"How is that possible?" I asked. "They have magic."

"So do you," she said.

"I don't know how to use it," I said.

"And they don't know how to live without it," she replied.

"Is that how you got away?" I asked. "Did you use magic?"

"Not magic, child, no. I got away because of kindness." She poured tea into a cup in front of me and steam swirled up from the cup, the scent of roses hanging in the air just as they had been in my bath.

Looking away from the cup, I returned my gaze to Nani. "What do you mean you escaped because of kindness?"

She held up the half eaten cake. "Every week, I made these for you when your father left for his trip to the markets. Every week, I made sure I made enough to send cakes to all the servants and guards in the house. The guard who was supposed to make sure I didn't get away, left the door unlocked for me. I slipped away quietly and went straight for the woods, hoping you had done the same."

"You didn't even have to use magic?" It wasn't really a question, but it came out like one.

"There is much you can do without magic," she said. "Now, eat. The servants are abuzz. The council sent out the first trial last night. Yours will arrive anytime now."

My stomach twisted into knots and the sweetness of the cake in my mouth turned dry and flavorless. I forced myself to swallow. Today Queen's Trial would officially begin. "What are the trials like?"

"It depends," she said. "The current council creates the challenges and sends them to each candidate. Not even the Queen herself knows what they are until they reach the candidates."

"How will I know what to do?" I asked. "Am I allowed to ask for help?"

"You'll find out soon enough," Nani said. "I was there when your mother went through her trials. She was just as nervous as you are and she flew through them. I have a feeling you'll do well, too."

"But she had years of training and grew up here," I said.

"She also could only channel magic from the Autumn Court.

You, on the other hand, will be able to channel magic from multiple courts."

A lump settled in my throat. It was true that I had the magic of all four courts, but that wasn't easing my anxiety. If anything, I had a feeling it might make things more difficult for me. Aside from being seen as a threat by the other candidates, I wasn't sure how that was possible but the nagging sense of dread wouldn't subside.

A knock on the door made me jump and I dropped the uneaten pastry on my plate. My pulse raced as Nani gracefully walked to the door to allow entry to whoever was on the other side. Was it time for the trial already? I squeezed my hands together in my lap, noting how damp my palms were. I hoped the anticipation of what was coming was worse than the actual trial.

A guard stood at the door, a small wooden box in his hands. Wordlessly, he passed the box to Nani. Then, he turned and left.

Nani cradled the box in her hands as if it would shatter if she so much as breathed on it. Carefully, she set the box on the table in front of me and let out a breath. She seemed just as nervous as me in that moment.

I licked my lips and moved my plate to the side before gently moving the box in front of me. On the top of the box, in large looping letters was my name. Under my name were the words *First Trial*.

I held my breath as I carefully unclasped the lid.

Chapter Fourteen

✢✢✢

The room was silent as I lifted the lid of the wooden box, allowing it to hang by its hinges. Inside was a bundle of light blue cloth that seemed to be covering something. Feeling both relieved and terrified that I had a moment longer before revealing the contents, I took a deep breath before lifting the fabric. Inside, I found a silver circle that looked like a bracelet.

Brow furrowed, I picked up the delicate metal ring and inspected it. There was no inscription. Frowning, I set the bracelet down and pulled the fabric out of the box. There was nothing more inside. No instructions, no other objects. Just a piece of blue fabric and a silver bangle. I stared at the bracelet as if it was going to come to life or give me a clue. It sat there, an innocent piece of metal on the table.

"I'll give you some time alone," Nani said.

"What am I supposed to do with this?" I asked, picking up the circle.

"You'll figure something out," she said.

I slouched into the chair, feeling defeated before I'd even begun. Lazily, I spun the bracelet around my finger on the table top, wondering if I was missing something. Was there some kind of magic I was supposed to use to unlock this thing? Was it all just a trick to see how I'd react? I looked up toward the door, wondering if I should chase Nani down. Then, thinking better of it, I let out a sigh and slipped the bracelet over my hand.

An icy chill, so cold it nearly burned, spread up my arm causing me to gasp. I looked down to see that the metal of the bracelet was expanding, climbing up my arm like liquid silver. Panic surged through me and I clawed at the cold creeping up my arm, trying to pull it off. The metal continued to expand, slithering its way up my arm to my shoulder and spreading across my chest. I tugged on the place where the bracelet had been, trying to pull it free of my arm but I couldn't grab hold of anything. My hand slipped on the cold, hard silver that had encased my lower arm.

The silver liquid hardened as it climbed, but the rate of progress seemed to slow. I took a steadying breath and looked around the room, trying to find some way of appeasing the growth. When I glanced back at the molten silver, it was no farther across my chest than it had been. The act of maintaining my composure must have halted its progress.

Focusing all my mental energy on remaining calm, I walked to the wardrobe and found a robe. Carefully, I pulled the sleeve over my unmoving sliver coated arm, then tugged the rest of the robe on, tying it around my waist. While Nani had excused herself, there was no specific indication that I couldn't ask for help. I cringed at the thought of finding Tristan with this problem, already anticipating the laughter that would accompany his discovery of my blunder. However, the Queen herself had suggested I go to him for help. I didn't think this was what she had in mind, but I knew I didn't have any other options.

Keeping my breathing even and my chin high, I opened the door to my room and stepped into the hallway.

The guards flanking either side of my door glanced at me, but didn't break their positions of attention. I paused in front of them. "Excuse me. Do you know where I could find the prince?"

One of the guards turned to face me. "He's likely in his study. I can take you there if you like, my Lady."

"Thank you," I said.

Silently, I followed the guard down the long hall and down a flight of stairs. We passed a formal dining room and several closed doors before turning down a few more hallways. I was grateful for the guide through the maze that was the Winter Palace. The castle was a labyrinth of hallways and ballrooms and dining halls. Too many of them looked the same to me to ever find my way around on my own without a map.

Finally, we stopped in front of an unassuming door with a brass doorknob. The guard knocked.

Rustling on the other side of the door let me know that the guard's guess as to Tristan's whereabouts was likely correct. The door swung open and Tristan's face appeared. His hair hung loose around his face in unkempt strands and his eyes looked tired. I'd never seen him so weary before.

My brow furrowed in concern and I forgot for a moment why I was here. All I wanted to do was help Tristan. A sharp pain on my side quickly tore me away from my worry for him and I winced.

The weariness in his expression melted away as his eyes widened and he moved toward me. "What's wrong?"

Wrapping his arm around me, Tristan guided me into his study and closed the door behind us. He didn't let me explain before he tore the robe off of me. Then he laughed.

I frowned. That wasn't the reaction I hoped for. Glancing down at my arm I noticed that the pain had come from the metal spreading under my arm and down my side. I looked back up at Tristan. "It's not funny. It keeps getting worse."

"I can fix it for you if you like," he said, extending a hand toward me.

I flinched, and backed away. "It's the first trial. I don't think I should have you do it for me."

He lowered his hand. "As you wish."

The cold metal pinched the skin on my neck and another surge of panic shot through me. What if it covered my face? I wouldn't be able to breathe. Could this material kill me? Eyes pleading, I looked at Tristan. "I need help, but don't do it for me. Teach me."

Tristan shrugged. "I can if you like but it would be much faster if I do it for you. You do realize that sometimes it's okay to ask for help. Even Queens need help on occasion."

I shook my head. There had been no instructions, but this was my trial. How would it look if I got kicked out after the first one?

"Well, you're going to have to use Winter magic. That's sea silver. It responds to heat. The more you move and the more your emotions flair, the worse it's going to get. You need cold to make it stop."

I didn't wait for any more instructions. I was in the Winter Court and I knew outside had to be colder than it was in here. I took off at a run down the hall and back the way the guard had taken me. Every step I took made my heart pound harder and with each step, the sea silver crept closer to my mouth, wrapping its way around my neck.

My throat felt tight and I wasn't sure if breathing was getting more difficult for real or if my fear was causing me to feel the constriction in my airway. Either way, I had to get to an exit.

I turned and found myself in a dead end. A hallway that went to nowhere. How was I supposed to find the exterior doors in this maze of a castle?

"Cassia," Tristan called. "Are you sure you don't need help?"

The sea silver was climbing up my chin. I touched my finger-tips to it and realized it was going to be over my mouth before I could get outside. Asking Tristan for help might cost me the trial, but if I didn't get help, I might lose my life.

"Cassia?" Tristan called again.

I couldn't see him, but I turned toward the sound of his voice. "Tristan. I need help. Please make it stop."

I gasped one last breath as the cold metal slithered over my lower lip, knowing I was running out of time. "Tristan!"

Tristan turned the corner and rushed to my side. Gently he touched his fingers to the layer of silver that was covering my lips and the burning cold of the metal stung as if it were on fire beneath his touch.

He dragged his fingers down my chin, over my neck, and along my shoulder, leaving a stinging trail of sparks in his wake. A moment later, the metal began to recede and I took a deep breath as relief rushed through me.

Tristan dragged his fingertips down my arm and encircled my wrist with his large hand, making me feel frail by comparison. The circle of sea silver slipped off of my wrist and landed with a ping on the floor.

My lower lip trembled as I stared at the object I'd thought of as harmless. I'd failed my first trial. How had I managed to mess things up so much in such a short time?

"I take it there's no such thing as sea silver in the human world?" Tristan asked.

I shook my head. "What am I going to do now?"

"You'll recount your experience and send the letter to the priests," Tristan said. "It's out of your hands. They make the final decision."

"Would it have worked if I made it outside in time?" I asked.

"No," Tristan said. "It has to be broken with internal cold. The kind of cold that only comes from magic. You weren't meant to pass this trial."

My stomach twisted into knots. "What do you mean?"

"Only a Winter Fae could have passed this trial," he said.

"Do you think they were trying to get rid of me?" I asked, not really wanting the answer.

"It's possible," he said. "Though I think it's unlikely that the priests would care enough to get that creative with their trial. If they want you gone, they'll call you back to the Autumn Court and let the other candidates take care of you for them."

I swallowed, not liking the sound of that. "So now I write a letter and wait?"

He nodded, then winked. "Why don't you let someone else escort you to your room, though? I hate to have you wandering these halls for hours."

"Good idea," I said. "And thank you. For saving me."

"You know you're of no use to me if you're dead."

"There's the Tristan I know," I said. "I was worried. For a minute there, I thought you actually cared about me."

Tristan pressed his lips together, but didn't respond. Instead, he turned away from me and looked at his guards. "Take her back to her room."

Chapter Fifteen

Feeling a little guilty for what I'd said to Tristan, I took advantage of his retreat to get away from him quickly. Some days, I wondered why I was so hard on him, but then I remember that he was the one who dragged me here to play a role in whatever game of politics he was currently engaged in.

I followed the guards in silence as I wondered what else could go wrong. I'd clearly ruined the first trial, I was stuck in the Winter Court posing as Tristan's bride to be, and Tiana was still out there somewhere along with whoever else was interested in killing me because of my blood. I rubbed the back of my neck as we walked, suddenly feeling overwhelmed. Maybe I should just crawl back in bed and sleep until everything was done and over with. Maybe being in the Winter Court was the best thing for me even if my heart ached with desire for the princes I'd left behind.

The guards paused in front of my door, then opened it before taking their positions on either side. I didn't acknowledge them as I passed between them and closed the door behind me. I was too exhausted and confused to talk to anyone here. I longed for words of comfort from Ethan or playful banter from Dane. Even Cormac's bluntness would be welcome right now.

Heading for the bed with every intention of napping until someone dragged me away, I noticed something out of the corner of my eye. On the table where my breakfast had been, the box containing the sea silver bracelet was gone. In its place was a new box. This one looked to be made of thick paper and was pale pink in color.

Nervous flutters filled my stomach as I stepped toward the object. I blew out a breath of relief when I didn't see a trial number written on it. Instead, it simply had my name across the top in gold ink.

Hoping it was from Tristan and not part of the trials, I carefully opened it. Inside I found a pen and several pieces of pink parchment along with a pink sealed envelope with the word *candidate* written on the front.

Frowning, I pulled out the envelope and opened it, hoping I wasn't walking into another trap.

DEAR CANDIDATE,

After each trial you are to account your experiences exactly as they occurred on the provided paper by the end of the day of the trial. Then place the letter in the box and close it. The letter will be reviewed by the council. Expect to see a return letter the following morning. The pen will know if your words are truth.

The Trial Council

RELIEVED that the box didn't contain anything nefarious, I decided to sit down and pen my letter now. I had to let them know I failed eventually. I kept my letter polite and to the point as I retraced my steps in words. As I signed my name at the end of the letter, I found that I felt a sense of relief. There was something liberating about not hiding the failure. Folding the paper in half, I set it in the box and closed the lid.

The task was done. Now I would wait.

No longer feeling tired, I stood and walked to the door. My first instinct was to call for Tristan, but our parting words to each other still stung. Deciding it didn't matter where I went as long as there were distractions, I walked through the door.

I could feel the gaze of the guards on my back as I headed down the hall and after a few more steps, I could hear their movement behind me in soft rustles of fabric. Their footfalls were nearly silent on the rug, but I knew they were following me. I supposed I should be grateful. Tristan seemed confident that I was safe here, but I wasn't sure I was safe anywhere.

I thought about the trials as I walked, taking turns when the mood struck me, allowing myself to get lost in the palace. My agreement with Tristan had been to stay until the first three trials were complete. What would become of my promise if I failed the first trial and was dismissed from the trial altogether? Would I have to stay until Tristan felt my bargain had been fulfilled or would they dismiss me when the successful candidates had completed their trials?

A terrible thought made my chest tighten. Did the princes already know? Did the Queen already know? If I had failed, was there already another assassin on their way to finish me so I wasn't a threat to whoever won? I rubbed my forehead, trying to calm the swirling thoughts. There wasn't anything I could do until the response came from the council.

Soft music filtered down the hall from an open door ahead. It was gentle and sad. The melody drawing me in like a moth to a flame. I floated toward the sound, forgetting my worries as I let the music take over my movements. Pausing in front of the open door, I peeked inside to see Sasha plucking the strings of a large harp. Her fingers moved with rapid familiarity as if she were part of the instrument. Her eyes were closed and her frail body swayed gently in time with the movements of her arms. Holding my breath, I hung on every note as she played. The song seemed to be an extension of her and it felt like I was intruding on an intimate secret. I knew I should give her privacy, but I longed to hear more.

Sasha glanced up and caught my eye, her hands pausing on the strings. The last lingering vibration of the notes faded as she stared at me. Her startled expression faded into a smile and she inclined her head. "Come in. You don't have to stand out there."

Slowly I walked into the room. "You play beautifully."

"Thank you," she said, shifting on the bench. As she moved, the fabric of her dress pulled around her and I could see her thin frame. She had looked so full of life in Tristan's memory. Now, she was a shell of that girl. So frail that I feared a strong breeze would blow her away.

"Have you made amends with my brother?" she asked.

"I'm not sure what you mean," I said.

"I know he sprung some things on you and I'm sure you were not pleased." She turned away from the harp, facing a pair of chairs that waited nearby.

I took the gesture as an invitation and claimed one of the empty seats. "Your brother and I seem to always be at odds no matter the occasion."

She smirked. "It's good for him to have someone who won't back down. Especially with all the trouble my father is causing."

I waited in silence, hoping she'd elaborate. When she didn't speak, I thought of the most diplomatic way I could address the issue. "Did your father used to live here in the Winter Palace?"

She nodded. "He did. Until he was too unwell. He moved to our mountain home where he remained until last year."

"Where is he now?" I asked.

"Staying with one of the high lords. Fueling their desire for war with his ravings." She stood, a wisp of a woman, still elegant in her movements despite the fact that they seemed to trouble her.

I stood and reached for her, ready to offer my support.

She waved my hand away. "I can manage this distance. I'm not as fragile as I appear."

Nodding, I stepped back to the chair I'd been sitting in and reclaimed my place. She sat in the chair next to me. "It's the magic. Shortly after my test with Tiana, it started to fade. I'm afraid I have very little left. Without magic, we Fae do not fare well. In time, I'll lose all my magic and age like a human until I pass from this world."

I couldn't stop the gasp that escaped my mouth and I quickly adjusted my expression in an attempt to show concern rather than pity.

"Don't worry," Sasha said. "I've lived a long, happy life. And it will be happy again once my father is defeated."

"Is that Tristan's plan, then?" I asked.

"Yes," she said. "He had a vision of you. Did you know that?"

I shook my head. "He hasn't told me anything."

She frowned. "Always trying to protect those he cares about, that one. I'm sure he thinks sparing you the details is kind. But I can tell that you're like me. Knowing helps."

"Yes, it does. If he would just include me, then maybe I could help without being so angry at him." The words spilled out and I felt my cheeks heat.

Sasha laughed. "He can be infuriating at times."

"That's an understatement," I mumbled.

"Do you want to know what his vision was?" she asked.

I swallowed, suddenly nervous. Tristan had kept this from me but Sasha openly offered to share. Did I want to know? Would knowing make being stuck here easier? Would it make things worse? I thought to the failed trail and pressed my lips together. It wasn't as if the day could get much worse. "Yes."

"He saw you long before you arrived," she said. "He used to tell me stories of the Fae changeling who came to him in his dreams. He said she was the key to saving the Winter Court before we even knew what the threat was."

"How?" I asked.

"He didn't know it was you until you met, of course," she continued. "But he had visions of you here to help create a bond between humans and Fae. He saw you as the pivotal piece in saving the lives of thousands." She paused, her forehead creasing.

"What else?" I encouraged, ignoring the chill sweeping through me.

"He also had visions where you died. In Queen's Trial. At the Autumn Court."

I felt like the air had been knocked from my lungs.

"Sasha," Tristan's voice carried into the room, smooth and commanding. "Those were not your stories to tell."

I looked up at the Winter Prince and was surprised to see concern rather than anger in his expression.

"She needed to know, Tristan. You can't shelter her forever," Sasha said.

He sighed as he walked into the room. "I can't with you around. That's for sure." He looked at me. "So now you've met Sasha."

"Is it true?" I asked. "Is that why you agreed to help me? Why you dragged me here? To help you with your war?"

"Yes," Tristan said.

I wasn't sure how I felt about his quick answer. As much as he drove me crazy at times, I did have feelings for him. There were times I even thought he had feelings for me. Now, it turns out this was all planned before we even met. I was a pawn, another step that allowed Tristan to gain what he wanted. "Does that mean I'll die from the trials when I return to the Autumn Court?"

Tristan shook his head. "I'm not sure."

I stood. "I think I'd like to go back to my room. It was nice seeing you again, Sasha."

"Again?" Tristan asked.

I turned and walked toward the doors, knowing the guards would be waiting for me.

"You need to explain everything to her," Sasha said behind me.

I didn't stay to hear Tristan's response.

Chapter Sixteen

My mind reeled as I sat alone in my room. Every so often a creak or rustle of fabric outside my door made my pulse race in anticipation of Tristan's arrival. When nobody came, my shoulders sagged and I felt foolish for my hope. I didn't want to feel this pull to Tristan, but I couldn't help it. The more I found out about him, the less of a villain he became. I couldn't ignore the fact that I wasn't thrilled with the idea that he'd helped me because he needed me for his own plans, but if he was somehow keeping me safe from death by having me here, I couldn't argue that. I didn't want to die. I wanted to find a place I belonged and enjoy my life. Queen or not, I wanted to find my place in Faerie and settle down.

Tristan's naked form flashed in my mind and I could almost feel the heat of his body as he pressed himself against me. The vision was gone almost as quickly as it had appeared, leaving me feeling flushed and wanting. I clenched my thighs together and took a deep breath. I couldn't be thinking about sex right now. I needed to focus. No matter my attraction to Tristan, I knew it wasn't a good idea to get involved with him physically. It wasn't just the complications he brought, it was the complications he'd cause between myself and the three princes who already had my heart. I felt a sinking emptiness without them. Like a piece of me was lingering in the Autumn Court, waiting for my return. How much longer was I going to have to stay here?

A rustling sound came from outside the door and I turned toward it, allowing myself to hope it was Tristan even after all my attempts to keep him from my mind.

The door knob turned and flutters rose into my chest and my breathing grew rapid. What should I say to him? How should I act around him? Was he going to tell me the truth?

All thoughts of Tristan left my mind the second the visitor came into view. This wasn't Tristan. A tall Fae male in a black and silver uniform towered in the doorway. His gray eyes locked on me and a wicked grin spread across his lips.

I glanced down to see the guards who had been outside my door on the ground, red blood staining the rug under them. My heart raced and I leaped from the bed and backed away from the intruder.

Glancing behind me, I looked for any sign of escape. There was a window in my room, but I was several floors up and wasn't sure how a jump would impact me. Could a Fae survive such a fall? How much did immortality protect you?

"So you're the Queen's brat." The male's boots slammed the floor with each step. He walked with power and dominance instead of grace. There was no fluidity to his motions. He was steel and stone.

"What do you want with me?" I asked.

"I'm not going to hurt you," he said.

I glanced at the dead guards he'd left behind, then looked back up at him.

He followed my gaze then turned back to me. "They weren't going to let me through. If they had cooperated, I would have let them live."

I tucked my trembling hands behind my back, not wanting to

show the intruder that he was intimidating me. I thought back to the last time I'd been in trouble. Ethan had felt it. He'd come for me. *Ethan,* I called out to him, not knowing if the distance was too far.

"Who are you?" I asked, hoping to buy myself some time.

"I'm here to retrieve you for a meeting with the king," he said.

My mouth felt dry and I licked my lips, trying to come up with any excuse to stall the male in the hopes of someone coming to help me. Right now would have been an excellent time to use some defensive magic if I knew any. Cursing the Queen's Trial and its disruption to my magic training, I glanced at the box behind me. "Do you see this?"

"The box?" the male asked, brow furrowed.

"Yes. I'm a candidate in the Queen's Trial in Faerie and I'm favor bound to this palace until I complete the third trial. I made an agreement with the Winter Prince."

"That was foolish of you," the male said. "But I'm afraid you don't have any choice. I'm not here to make arrangements with you. I'm here to retrieve you." He crossed the room in three large steps. "You'll either come on your own, or I'll force you to come."

A gleam of silver caught my eye and I noticed he was holding a blade. I squeezed my hands into fists, my fingernails biting into my palms. I wondered what my chances for escape were if I tried my magic. Could I get by him in time to escape if I lit up the room?

Deciding it was my only hope, I searched for my magic, trying to find that thread that led to my power.

The male clicked his tongue. "You've never met a real Winter Guard before, have you?"

I swallowed hard and kept my eyes locked on his.

He smirked. "You can't use magic against me. Nobody with Winter magic can. And I hear you've got the magic of all four courts? Shame. If you were true Autumn Fae, you'd have a chance."

He held out his hand. "Are you coming with me or shall I report to the king that I found you with your throat slit when I arrived?"

I stared defiantly at him. I didn't know much about the Winter Court, but I believed Tristan and Sasha that the king was insane. I had no intention of going to meet him.

"Once I kill you, I'll find the princess and let her join you in death. Maybe I'll even go after the prince. I'm sure the king will forgive me if I kill him instead of saving the pleasure for him."

I narrowed my eyes at the guard, hatred rising in my gut making my skin burn. How dare he threaten Sasha and Tristan?

"Count of three, Princess," the guard said. "One, two..."

Lower lip trembling, I reached my hand toward his.

He wrapped calloused fingers around my hand, enclosing it in his. "That's better."

Before I could say anything, the room went black.

I dug my fingernails into the Winter Guard's hand, hoping he'd loosen his grip. He only squeezed my hand tighter. Twisting as much as possible, I tried to break his grip, but he held on. If I was thrown from the slide, I might have a chance to contact Ethan or at least seek shelter. All too soon, the light reappeared and I landed in a heap on a hard floor.

Pain shot out through my right hip where I'd landed and I rolled to my side, groaning. I hated sliding. Glaring up at the male, I bared my teeth. "You did that on purpose."

"You tried to escape," he said with a shrug.

I pushed myself to standing while rubbing my injured side and looked around. I was in a grand room appointed with luxurious details. The floor was black stone and the walls were covered in silver wallpaper. A gray rug ran down the center of the room from a large metal door up to a raised dias. On top of the dias was a silver and black throne. "Where are we?"

"The Mountain House," the Winter Guard said.

"He keeps a throne room like this in his second home?" I asked, not meaning to say the words out loud.

"This is the seat of power for the Winter Court," the guard said.

"What about the palace?" I asked.

"Where the traitors have taken up residence?" he asked.

"You mean his children?" I asked.

The door swung open and a silver-haired Fae male in a black tunic and sweeping silver cape strode into the room. He wore black trousers and black leather boots. His steps were even and steady. The male looked at me with icy blue eyes; the same eyes as Tristan. His jaw tightened as he walked toward me, not breaking eye contact.

When he reached the place where the guard and I stood, he stopped and clasped his black gloved hands in front of him. "Thank you for coming, Cassia."

I raised my eyebrows in surprise. "I wasn't given a choice."

"I apologize for that," he said. "I'm afraid you've been corrupted by my son and I needed to free you from his grasp."

I blinked at the male in front of me. "So you're the king."

He nodded. "Indeed. The one they all say is insane. Tell me, child. Do I look like I'm unfit to rule?"

It was a loaded question and I tightened my jaw, afraid to give the incorrect answer.

He smiled. "I know it's hard to understand, but believe me when I say I'm doing this for your protection."

"The guards," I said, "he killed them."

"I was unable to avoid injury during her retrieval," the Winter Guard said.

"That is unfortunate. But the important part is that you're safe now," the king said.

"Please, I can't be here. I'm participating in Queen's Trial. If you won't let me return to the Winter Palace, at least let me return to the Autumn Court." It was a desperate plea and I knew it was risky, but everything about the king made my stomach wreathe in distress. There was something about him that wasn't right even if he did come across as diplomatic and sane on the exterior. It was something that went beyond the fact that he'd had me kidnapped. Every bone in my body was screaming for me to get away from him. My instincts were on fire in protest.

"I'm afraid that isn't going to happen. However, we'll be happy to let the council know you are completing your trials here." The king inclined his head in what was meant to be an act of diplomacy.

Instead, my skin crawled at the sight. There was something very wrong with the Winter King.

Chapter Seventeen

I knew it was possible I wasn't even a candidate in the trials anymore, but something told me the only reason I was alive was because the king saw me as valuable. If I was no longer in the running to become Queen, would he care about my wellbeing?

Lifting my chin, I did my best to act the part of a future Queen. "The message box that allows me to communicate with the council was left behind."

"Don't you worry about that." He snapped his fingers and the door opened again.

A thin Fae female in gold robes glided into the room. Her gait was so smooth I wondered if she was floating. Her face was narrow and delicate with a thin nose and small, pointed ears. Her hair was slivery blue and reminded me of a pond near my father's house.

The female bowed at the king. "Your highness."

"Tell my guest what you told me," he said.

The female turned to me and pursed her lips. Her eyes flicked up and down my body as if assessing me. Then, she glanced from me to the king then back again.

My breath caught as I read her body language. She was as much a guest in this place as I was.

"Lady Cassia, it's an honor to meet you." The female inclined her head. "I am priestess Jaya, one of the members of the Trial Council."

My brow furrowed and I wanted to demand what she was doing here, but I held my tongue. If my suspicions were accurate, she didn't want to be here.

"I will provide you the communications necessary for your trials while you remain as an ambassador to the Winter Court." She turned to the king. "Sire, may I have a few minutes in private to discuss her first trail?"

"She's practically family," the king said. "I'm sure she won't want to hide anything from me. Isn't that right, princess?"

I bristled at the title. When Tristan called me *princess* it was irritating, but playful. When his father used it I had to force myself to keep from vomiting. Forcing the grimace on my face into a smile, I nodded. "Yes, I'm sure it's fine to share here."

Jaya let out a sigh and her shoulders sank. It made me wonder what she was hoping to say to me had we been granted privacy.

"You passed your first trial," she said.

Despite the circumstances, I blew out a breath of relief. "How?"

The king raised an eyebrow and I turned away from him, focusing on Jaya.

"You were not expected to be able to complete the first task. Each candidate was given a task that required magic they could not conjure. I have to admit, it was difficult to think of something we could use for you given your unique situation."

I frowned. "So everyone knows, then."

"They do," she said.

"You wanted us to fail?" I asked. "I could have died."

"One of the candidates did die," Jaya said. "Queen's Trial is not a game."

I covered my mouth with my hand. "Someone died?"

"Yes. A good ruler must know when help is required. She must know when there is something happening that is outside her control. For the first trial, you were required to identify that and seek help from a qualified source. You succeeded."

The death of the unknown candidate hung over me like a black cloud preventing me from finding joy in the fact that I'd passed. I stood motionless in silence, staring at the ground, unsure of how to proceed.

Jaya cleared her throat.

I looked up at her.

"Your second trial will begin tomorrow. I've made the proper arrangements for it to be sent here," she said.

"I knew I chose the right council member. Not only did you make it happen, you're ordained with the power of the gods. One of the few Fae who can perform a royal marriage. Isn't she amazing?" the king asked, turning to me.

My chest tightened. I had a feeling he wasn't interested in a marriage between his son and me. The king was obsessed with procreating with Fae from other courts in an attempt to gain heirs with multiple courts worth of magic. And here I was, the offspring of a Queen, holder of all four courts as passed down from my mother. Bile rose in my throat at the thought of the king attempting any physical contact with me. I had to get out of there.

"Rest tonight, my champion," the king said. "Tomorrow you will be one step closer to claiming the crown. And if you fail, don't worry. You'll always have a place here by my side."

I swallowed the sick feeling, unwilling to open my mouth to speak for fear that I'd lose the contents of my stomach. I'd never met someone so power hungry before. Even my human father had limits based in morality. I was pretty sure he wouldn't have stolen a female from anyone.

The door opened again and my heart thundered against my

ribs. I wasn't sure I could handle any more surprises today. A familiar figure walked through the door, chin held high. I let out a gasp of both relief and fear as Nani walked through the door. I ran toward her without waiting for permission.

She met me in an embrace, pulling me close until her mouth was up against my ear. "Just do what he says for now. We'll be out of here soon."

My jaw tightened at her words and I made the smallest nod I could against her before pulling away. "Are you hurt?"

She brushed the hair away from my eyes and smiled. "I'm the one who is supposed to ask you that question."

"My gift to you, princess," the king said. "I know how much she means to you so I had her brought here with you."

Teeth clenched, I did my best to not glare at him. After allowing myself a few deep breaths through my nose, I lowered my head. "Thank you, your highness."

The king laughed. "Now you're learning your place."

Heat rose to my cheeks and I squeezed my hands into fists behind my back to keep from speaking out. If not for Nani's words, I would have tried to flee. Or attack the king at the very least. My magic still felt muted, but the distance from the guard allowed me to feel the slightest inkling of it. I wondered if I'd be able to use it once we were deposited wherever they were going to place us.

"Take her to her room," the king said.

One of the guards grabbed my upper arm and I tugged it away. "I can walk myself."

The guard removed his hand and cleared his throat. "This way."

Nani took my hand in hers and we followed the Winter Guard.

THE WORD *ROOM* was used very liberally by the king. We weren't in the kind of room I was used to since arriving in Faerie. We were in a dungeon.

As soon as the guard closed the door behind us, I ran to it and tried the handle. Searing pain stung my palms and I let go of the handle, screaming.

Nani was by my side instantly, cradling my injured hand in hers. An angry red circle spread across my palm and up to the parts of my fingers that had touched the door knob.

"Iron," Nani said.

I looked up at the door. In addition to the black iron door knob, there was a small window with iron bars on the top of the door. I glanced around the rest of the room. We were walled in on all sides by gray stone. One small iron barred window was our only source of light. In one corner, a wooden bench was pushed against the wall. A folded blanket sat on one end of it. On the other side was a small table with a basin of water and a hand towel. A single chair took up the corner nearest the door.

Pulling my hands away from Nani, I walked back toward the door.

"Cassia, stop!" Nani called.

I ignored her and stood on my tiptoes to peer out of the window, bracing myself against the wooden door as I looked to avoid touching the iron bars. Torchlight flickered in the dark hall. Beyond our room I saw what looked to be a hallway with at least three more doors that looked like ours.

"Hello? Anyone out there?" I called into the darkness. Turning my ear toward the window, I listened for a response. After several minutes standing frozen by the door, I realized we were either alone or nobody could hear us.

"Cassia," Nani said. "What are you doing?"

I turned back to her. "Checking to see if we're alone."

"I think we are," Nani said. "From what I heard, the king doesn't have a lot of his guards with him."

"That's good," I said. "Now, tell me everything. I mean every-thing. Please."

Nani sighed. "Where do you want me to start?"

"Why not start where we left off and work your way back?" I asked. "Start with how you got here."

"Alright," she said. "I was in the servants' quarters when a large Winter Guard showed up. He told me he'd taken you and that I could either come freely or die. I came freely."

My brow furrowed. "Why didn't you fight?"

"I did what was best," she said. "There were other servants nearby. They heard everything. I knew if I left quietly, that they'd be left alone. I'm sure they went to the prince to tell him what happened the second we were gone. I haven't been there long, but I learned quickly how fiercely loyal the prince's household is to him. And the loyalty already extends to you."

I swallowed, my mouth dry. She hadn't even put up a fight in the hopes that someone would be able to get word to Tristan. Nani had cared for me since I was a child and she was still looking out for me without any thought to her own wellbeing. This wasn't the act of a monster or a creature who was evil. My father had thrown her out because he thought she'd healed me. Humans were so afraid of magic. I shook my head. "You don't have to keep sacrificing so much for me, you know."

"That's what we do for those we love, Cassia."

I stepped away from the door and wrapped my arms around her. "Thank you, Nani. For everything."

She hugged me back and kissed the top of my head. "It's been a pleasure watching you grow and I'm not about to give up on you now."

I pulled away from Nani. "So now what?"

She pressed her palm against my cheek. "You need to call to Ethan. You two have a bond. He will hear you and he will come."

I tensed at her words. "I don't want him to be in danger. I don't want any of them in danger. This isn't just about my safety, it's about Queen's Trial, and a war in the Winter Court. They can't be part of it."

"Sometimes you need help, Cassia. The king is unstable. The longer we stay here, the more at risk you are," she said.

"Isn't there another way?" I asked.

"Cassia," Nani chided.

"Nani, I know there are times I need help. But I'm not willing to put them at risk for me. They've all risked enough for me."

"What about Tristan?" she asked.

"We're not bonded," I said. "I can't connect with him."

"You can connect with your mate," she said.

"I have a mating bond with Ethan," I said.

She lifted an eyebrow. "Just Ethan?"

My stomach twisted into knots as I thought about all of the princes. I felt a connection to all of them. Even Tristan.

"There are different ways you feel the bond," she said. "I've seen the way he looks at you. I've seen the way he treats you."

"Like I'm only tolerable when I'm of use to him," I said.

"Like he's afraid you're going to leave him," she said.

"He doesn't do that. He acts as if he wants me to go. He doesn't let me get close to him. Every time I feel like we're making progress, he says something to push me away." My throat tightened as I thought about all the times we'd connected, only to have one of us hurt the other.

"It's worth a try," Nani urged. "I don't see how else we'll get out of here before the king does something permanent."

Chapter Eighteen

I paced the room, considering Nani's words. Was it possible that Tristan and I had a mating bond? I found myself drawn to him and desiring him, but I couldn't let myself act on those thoughts. I'd seen visions of the two of us together and there was a part of me that ached for them to come true. But I was risking everything with the other princes if I did anything with Tristan. I knew how much they disliked each other. Cormac especially.

My heart felt like it was being squeezed at the thought of Cormac finding out that I had romantic feelings for Tristan. What would that do to him? He had finally opened up to me and I feared it would undo everything.

Even as I worried about the others, Tristan crept into my thoughts. It was possible he was already on his way to me. The corners of my vision blurred and something tugged at my resolve. I felt as if I was trying to remember something from long ago. I stopped walking and let my mind go blank.

Images of Tristan filled my mind and instead of pushing it away, I let it come. I could see him walking through a hallway in the Winter Palace, a determined expression on his face. He was flanked by two other figures, but they were blurry and I couldn't make out their details. I wanted to call out to him, to grab his arm and pull him to me. *Tristan*, I called to him in my head. As much as I pushed him away and as much as I vilified him, Tristan made me feel safe. I knew Nani was right. I needed his help.

Tristan paused in the hallway and looked up as if he had heard my silent cry. I tensed as an icy chill grabbed hold of me, working its way through my veins. If we were connected, if he could hear me...What if Nani was right?

Tristan, I tried again. *I need help. I'm with your father at his mountain house. Please. I don't know what to do.*

I watched his temples bulge as his jaw tightened, then he started moving again and I lost him.

Feeling exhausted, I staggered to the nearest wall and slid down until I was sitting on the cold, stone floor.

"What happened?" Nani asked.

"I think I reached him," I said.

"Good." She sat down next to me and wrapped her arm around my back, easing my head onto her chest. "You should rest. We don't know how long it will take."

I wanted to argue with her. I wanted to find a way out of this on my own, but as I breathed in Nani's familiar vanilla and honey scent, I realized how tired I was. I didn't want to wait to be rescued, but maybe the first trial had taught me a lesson. There were times when you needed help.

CREAK.

I opened my eyes and sat up straight, the sound of the door opening instantly waking me. My heart thundered in my chest and I pushed myself to standing. Nani rose next to me and she stepped in front of me as our visitor was revealed.

The petite Fae member of the council, Jaya, was standing in the opening. Behind her was another Winter Guard. His massive figure dwarfed the female. Her posture was hunched, her shoulders practically at her ears. Clearly, she was just as afraid to be here as I was. Probably more.

I moved away from Nani and smiled at Jaya, trying to ease some of her discomfort. "Good morning," I said. "To what do we owe the pleasure of your visit?"

Jaya inclined her head. "I've come to deliver your second trial."

I sucked in a breath. "So soon?"

She nodded and held out rolled yellow parchment, tied with a green ribbon.

I walked over to her and extended my hand. She passed me the roll of parchment.

"It isn't going to be easy completing my trial from a dungeon cell," I said.

"You'll manage," the Guard said from behind Jaya.

"You have everything you need to complete this trial on you," Jaya said. "I made sure of that."

"She'll return at the end of the day to see how you did," the Guard said. Then, he tugged Jaya away from the door and slammed it shut.

I winced at the sound of the door and turned away from it, worried my expression could be read as fear toward the guard. I looked down at the paper in my hand. It was small, the size of a letter. Yet, it felt heavy in my hand. I wasn't prepared for another trial. Especially not as a captive by a stranger. How was I going to complete this? I'd hardly even passed the first trial.

With a sigh, I walked over to the bench and sat down. I looked up at Nani who had settled into the chair nearby. "What if I can't figure it out this time?"

"I'm sure you will," she said.

"What if I do?" I asked.

Silence hung between us. I could tell she knew what I was asking. There was a reason the Winter King was holding me here.

We hadn't discussed it yet, but it was clear. He'd tried to take over all of Faerie once before. By capturing me, he was either attempting to get to my mother, the current Queen, or he was trying to hold on to the future Queen. Or worse, he wanted me to fail so he could attempt to get an heir off of me. None of those options boded well for me and I'd rather die than end up as a prisoner here.

"You still have the third trial and the three trials at the Autumn Palace. You can't win from here. He'll have to let you go on to the next stage if he wants you to win," she said.

"What if he's trying to get to my mother?" I asked. "Or what if he wants me to fail?"

"You can't worry about anyone else right now. Captured or not, you still have to pass the second trial or you will be out. There's a time limit and it doesn't hold for anybody."

I bit down on my cheek, forcing back all the things I wanted to say about how unfair this whole thing was. The thoughts swirling through my head were childish and unbecoming a Queen. Queens had to deal with far worse than my current situation.

Taking a deep breath, I found my resolve. I was going to solve this trial, then I would find a way out of here. Perhaps I could convince them to let me use a library or sitting room for the third trial if I was still awaiting rescue. Perhaps I could escape on my own. I frowned at the thought, knowing that Nani would be left behind. I couldn't do that to her again. I knew it wasn't like escaping the human realm. If I left her here, I'd never see her again.

Before I could tug on the ribbon to open the scroll, the door opened again. I turned, unsure of what to expect.

A younger Fae male in the Winter Guard uniform walked in with a tray of food. He had blond hair pulled back at the base of his neck and blue eyes. He set it down on the floor in front of the door. "Breakfast."

My brow furrowed as I studied him. He looked familiar, but I couldn't place it. Just as he was closing the door, it hit me. "Wait!"

I handed the scroll to Nani and I bolted to the door, sidestepping the tray of food. The guard paused at the door, peering through a crack the width of my hand. "Yes?"

"Why are you here? Why aren't you with Tristan and Sasha?" I asked.

The male's eyes widened.

"You don't have to do what he says, you know," I said. "You can leave. I'm sure Tristan would welcome you."

"With Tristan gone, I'm the eldest son," he said, then he closed the door.

My shoulders dropped. Tristan had mentioned siblings, but the only ones I'd seen were Sasha and Anya. Were his other siblings here too? Did he know they were here supporting his father?

"Cassia." Nani held out the scroll. "Now's not the time to dwell. You must complete the trial."

I pressed my palms into my temples, easing the pain that had started in my head. We'd only been gone one night, but already I missed the warmth and comfort of the Winter Palace. It made me feel weak. I didn't want to feel weak. Dropping my hands to my side, I rolled out my shoulders and walked to Nani. Everything was so uncertain right now, but there was still a task that needed done.

Nani lifted the scroll away from me. "Promise me one thing first."

"Anything," I said.

"If you have a chance to run, to be safe from here, you take it."

"Nani, I can't leave you again," I said.

"You know I can take care of myself," she said. "Promise me."

I nodded.

She lowered the scroll. "Good luck."

"Thank you." Taking the scroll, I pulled off the ribbon and

unrolled it. My brow furrowed as I read the single word in the middle of the parchment. *Wisdom.*

I looked up at Nani, a question on my lips. Then, the room dissolved, Nani slipping away from me.

Suddenly, I was standing in the middle of a forest. Thousands of tall pine trees as far as the eye could see. Dappled sunlight covered the floor of pine needles. I was still holding the scroll and I glanced at it again only to see a new word in the middle of the parchment. *Survive.*

Chapter Nineteen

C hills ran down my spine. Jaya had mentioned that one of the candidates had died in the first trial. Now, my new trial was to literally stay alive. I knew Queen's Trial was going to be difficult, and I knew I'd face risks. But I'd thought those risks would come from outside sources. I thought I had to stay clear of the other candidates and any other enemies. The males that had tried to get information from me and Tiana's threats seemed so far away as I stood alone, surrounded by trees.

I didn't have a destination or direction to travel. I didn't have a weapon or supplies. The back of my throat stung as fear crept through me. It reminded me of my arrival in Faerie. I'd been chased by horrible monsters and forced to survive on my own for a few hours.

Then, the fear that had started as a trickle took hold, squeezing my chest until I struggled to breathe. This wasn't just about survival for me. With all four courts worth of magic, I was at risk of drawing out the creatures from the Under. Being out in the open like this was a death trap.

I had to get out of there, but there was no clue as to the objective. Was I supposed to find my way somewhere or simply survive in here? I looked down at the parchment, hoping for more information but this time, it was blank.

Frustrated, I crumbled the useless document in my hand and shoved it in an inner pocket of my dress. Why must I have decided to wear something that was so poorly designed for survival?

Cursing my thin shoes, I started walking, trying my best to avoid the rocks and pinecones on the ground. Water. I needed to find water. I knew that was both my best bet for getting out of here and the necessary item I needed to live if I were here for a long time.

I wasn't a hunter. I'd never been trained as one. All I had was my intuition and a basic sense of geography. I remembered what Cormac had said about tracking and Autumn magic. It was possible I could harness it and help guide me through, but I would risk exposing too much magic if I did. Then, I remembered something about using my magic being beneficial. There was so much I still didn't know.

I stopped for a moment, taking a deep breath and closing my eyes. I needed to channel my magic and cycle it so it stayed at the surface. It was possible I'd need it. But I decided right then and there, I'd save it for an emergency. If a creature found me or I was under a threat, I would have enough to escape. If I used it now to try to navigate, I didn't know how much I would waste or how it would even work. I knew magic took time to recharge and for now, I was safe.

Shaking out my hands and wiggling my fingers, I fought against the chill the shadows brought. If I was still here by nightfall, it might be emergency enough to attempt my Summer magic at the very least. I was going to freeze out here.

Whatever I did, I needed to get back to Nani quickly. I didn't like the idea of her being alone with the Winter King. Eyeing the landscape, I turned in the direction that appeared to have a downward slope and began my search for water. All I could do was hope I was making the right choices.

A branch crunched under my footsteps, sending animals scurrying away from the sound. I didn't see any of the creatures living here, but I could hear birdsong and chittering along with occasional rustling. None of the sounds seemed out of place or like they belonged to anything especially large.

I rubbed my hands along my arms, warming myself. At least I'd been in the Winter Court and my dress was long sleeved. Had I been in a more formal gown or in a warmer court when they whisked me away to this place, I'd be in trouble.

Something large rustled the trees to my right. I turned to see whole branches swaying as a figure came crashing through.

Hands out in front of me, I called to my magic, letting it rise to the surface in a hum. The figure collapsed to the ground and I lowered my hands. This wasn't a monster. It was a Fae female in a thin, sparkling gown that probably used to be pink. Now, it was torn and covered in dirt. From her clothing, she appeared to be from a well to do family. The female was face down, her auburn braids were nearly undone and twigs and debris stuck out of her hair making it look more like a bird's nest than the hair of a proper female.

I knelt down just as she looked up from the ground. Her pale face was dusted with freckles and dirt was smudged on her cheeks and forehead. Green eyes looked up at me, brow furrowed. I offered my hand. "Are you alright?"

The female pushed back, away from me. She was shaking like an animal who had been abused.

I extended my hand again. "I won't hurt you."

She scooted herself back again until she bumped into the back of a tree.

"Are you one of the candidates?" I asked. "My name is Cassia."

The female's eyes narrowed as she studied me. I waited

patiently, my outstretched hand still hanging in the space between us.

"You're the one they're all talking about," she said, her voice small and almost squeaky.

"Probably," I said, raising my eyebrows and lifting my offered hand. "Do you need help?"

She let out a long breath and her shoulders sagged. Then, she finally reached for my hand.

I pulled her up as I stood and I took in the full sight of her. Her thin dress had been made of what I guessed was satin that only covered her breasts and her upper thighs. The rest of her dress was a sheer lace with a delicate flower pattern. What survived of it was in tatters, torn across her midsection and dangling in pieces from her shoulders. She had to be freezing.

"Where are you from?" I asked.

"Spring Court," she said. "House Valoi."

"Second trial?" I asked.

She nodded. "Wasn't expecting to be dropped into the middle of the forest."

"Tell me about it," I said.

"You didn't know in advance?" she asked.

I scoffed. "Why would I know about it in advance?"

The female shrugged. "That's what they're saying. That you are already chosen to win. They said the only way we could win was if we eliminated you."

I took a step back from the female. She seemed frail and delicate. Not the type you'd expect to pull a weapon from her skirts, but I'd learned not to let anything surprise me in Faerie.

"Don't worry," she said. "I don't have any weapons. Besides, I don't even want to be Queen to be honest."

My brow furrowed. "I don't understand. If you don't want to be Queen, then why would you go through all this?"

She smiled. "I'm the eldest daughter of House Valoi. We haven't had a Queen in our house for several generations. I'm sort of obligated to keep the family name and all. I guess you don't have to worry about that, do you?"

I swallowed and looked down for a moment. I didn't really have a family name. At least not anymore. I'd had one in the human realm, but that didn't belong to me.

"I'm Malin," the female said.

I looked up at her. "Nice to meet you, Malin."

"Well," she took a deep breath and glanced around, "I suppose I should get going."

"Do you know where you're going?" I asked before I realized she probably wouldn't share if she knew.

She laughed. "No idea. I've just been walking toward the sun. At least, I think it's the direction of the sun."

"We could help each other," I suggested. "There's nothing in the rules that I know of that says we have to work alone."

She lifted an eyebrow. "The first trial did reward us for asking for help. And I don't want the throne."

"We're not enemies here," I said. "There's no reason we can't work together."

She smiled, then shivered, moving her arms around herself. "Whatever we're going to do, we should do it quickly. I wasn't dressed for a journey."

I thought my dress was bad, but Malin had clearly come from somewhere much warmer. We both needed to get out of here before nightfall. My stomach growled and I pressed my hand against it. I hadn't eaten in a while. That was another reason to get out of these woods. "Any ideas what they want us to do here?"

She shook her head. "I was hoping you got some insight."

"None," I said, tempted to tell her that until the trial had sent me here, I'd been a prisoner. I didn't know her well enough yet for that. "It sounds like you were trying to get out of the woods, right?"

"Yes," she said. "I don't want to be here when it gets dark.

Who knows what creatures might come out at night? Especially if anything breaks free of the Under." She shuddered.

A wave of guilt cascaded through me. If anything from the Under found us, I knew it would be because of me. Though, I had a feeling Malin wouldn't survive on her own even if monsters never attacked. "I was looking for water. In my studies, I was taught that towns and cities were built near large water sources. If we can find a stream, it might lead us to a river."

"I saw a stream when I first arrived here. But I've been walking for a while now." She turned in a slow circle as if trying to remember which direction she'd come from.

"You said you were traveling toward the sun, right?" I asked.

She nodded.

"Let's try to go away from the sun and see if we can find your stream," I said.

She shivered again and rubbed her hands on her bare arms. "Sounds good. Anything to get us out of here and into a warm house."

We started walking, weaving around trees and the occasional boulder. The call of birds and rustle of branches overhead seemed to travel with us as the smaller creatures of the woods observed us from their hiding places. A soft pine scented breeze blew past us and the shadows of the trees grew longer as we walked making the sunlight more scarce with each passing minute. I wondered if we were nearing sunset or if it was cloudy. Looking up, I tried to find patches of sky, but the overgrowth was so wild it was difficult to catch more than a small piece of sky. It was difficult to find the sun as we walked so I made sure I kept us moving down the slope, going toward the lowest point. Hopefully, we'd find water soon.

Malin's skin was taking on a purplish tint as the temperature dropped and I worried that she was going to get ill from the cold. I didn't have any way of warming her without attempting to build a fire and that would slow us down more than I'd like. "You're from the Spring Court?" I asked, trying to come up with ways to distract her.

"Yes," she said.

"What's it like there?" I asked.

"Warm," she said with a bitter laugh. "And beautiful. Flowers everywhere. The most pleasant company, and the best food."

I smiled as I watched her face light up with warmth for her home. "It sounds wonderful."

"It really is," she said.

"Tell me more about Spring Fae," I said, thinking of Ethan. My heart ached as I longed to see him, to be in his arms.

"What do you want to know?" she asked.

"Anything, really," I said. "Your favorite festival. Something to make us think of a happier time and place."

She paused in her step for a moment and her eyes looked a little misty, as if she were about to cry. Then she blinked and resumed walking. I kept pace with her, staying on her side as I continued to check the sky for signs of the sun.

"The Spring Solstice, of course," she said. "As I'm sure it's the Autumn Equinox where you're from."

I forced a smile on my lips at her comment. She seemed to know who I was and what I was capable of, but she didn't know I was raised in the human realm. No wonder the candidates thought I was so powerful. If they believed I'd been raised in Faerie and trained in all four courts of magic, they were probably terrified of me. I wondered if I should tell her where I was from, ease some of her fear. But I wasn't sure if it was better to have my competition fear me.

"Every year we prepare for weeks," she said. "My family has six greenhouses where we grow hyacinth, and tulips, and daffodils. We use thousands of flowers for the festival. Every table is covered in flowers. And we deliver bouquets to the families that live on our lands. It's tradition to bring in good fortune and fertility."

"It sounds amazing," I said. "I'd like to see it one day."

"Win," she said matter of factly.

"I'm sorry?" I turned and looked at her, startled by her response.

"The Queen oversees the seasonal festivals in every Court, not just the Autumn Court," she said. "If you win, you'll have to come. You can stay with me. I'd be honored to host you."

"You don't even know me," I said. "Let alone know if I'd be a good Queen."

"I heard you have the support of the Spring Prince. I've known Ethan a long time. If he believes in you, I do too."

Warmth spread through me at her support. It seemed genuine and she gave it without expectation of reciprocation. I wanted to hug her.

A low growl sounded ahead and the underbrush rustled. Something large was waiting for us. And it was about to pounce.

Chapter Twenty

A griffin crept forward through the underbrush, its head and shoulders lowered while its rear was up in the air. The creature looked wound like a spring about to explode. I held my breath as flashes of my encounter with Tiana wrestled for my attention. I knew I needed to act but what did you do to fight a griffin?

Malin grabbed my upper arm, squeezing so hard I felt her nails bite into my skin. "Cassia." Her voice shook as she continued to squeeze my arm. "What do we do?"

I knew running wasn't an option and that any second the creature was going to pounce. My mind whirred and I felt my magic rise in the pit of my stomach where I'd left it after cycling it when I'd first arrived. This wasn't the first time I'd let my magic do its thing so releasing it wasn't the worst idea. As if agreeing with my decision, the magic clawed inside me, desperate to escape. I tugged Malin's hand off of my arm and closed my fingers around hers. Then, I forced everything I had toward the griffin.

Wind rushed past us, blowing my hair around my face and blocking my eyes. I heard the griffin growl. I brushed my hair away from my eyes and squinted into the rushing wind. The griffin was standing upright now, staring at me with its teeth bared. Small branches whipped past me, then a baby tree that was uprooted flew at us.

I dragged Malin down and squatted on the ground as the tree flew past us and made contact with the startled griffin. The creature yelped, then took off in the opposite direction from us. I blew out a breath and the tension eased just as the wind died down.

Malin turned and looked at me, her face drained of color. "What was that?"

"A griffin," I said. "Come on, we should get out of here before the monster brings his friends."

We turned away from the monster and headed the opposite direction. I stopped a few steps into our new course as a sharp pain shot from my chest to my side. I clutched at my side and turned to see that Malin was doing the same thing. "What was that?"

"Magic," Malin said. "Something powerful must be nearby. We should probably turn back. I don't want to run into whatever that could be."

"Unless," I paused, thinking about the warm buzz that radiated through my whole body. It was like an echo to the magic I felt when I channeled my magic. "What if that's what we're here for. What if we're supposed to find that magic?"

She rubbed her arms, battling the cold again now that the adrenaline had worn off. "If you want to go, I'll go with you."

"I think it's our best bet," I said. "It's the first sign of direction we've had since we arrived. What if the griffin was sending us away? What if it was a hint?" Again, I thought about Tiana's griffins and how they seemed like they'd been trained. Was it possible there were others who had taught the creatures how to do their bidding?

"Let's go," Malin agreed. "What do we have to lose?"

I released my magic, letting it flow through me instead of

holding it back. A gentle tingling radiated through me. The magic was no longer clawing to escape. For the first time, I felt like I was in harmony with my magic.

Nearby, I felt a pulse that mirrored the feeling of magic. It seemed to draw us in. I turned toward it, then paused to look at Malin. She had turned the same direction as if she could feel it too. The two of us moved forward, quietly as we could through the underbrush.

The temperature dropped again as we lost more sunlight. Soon we wouldn't be able to see in the shadows that were claiming the woods. Neither of us spoke as we walked toward the feeling. I thought Malin was just as ready to leave this place as I was.

We wove around an especially large tree and then we both stopped. My jaw dropped open as I stared at a glowing gem in front of us. It hovered above the ground, letting off warmth and a gentle hum. I moved closer, feeling some of the tension melt off of me as the gem warmed my frozen limbs.

Malin reached her hands out toward it, warming them in the glow as if she were in front of a hearth. "Now what?"

"I think we're supposed to take it. Or at least touch it," I said.

"You first, if it's a competition, I don't want to win," she said.

My brow furrowed, still finding it difficult to understand why she was here if she didn't want to win. But I knew family pressure was difficult to avoid. "What if we touch it at the same time? If this thing gets us out of here, I don't want you left here freezing all night."

"Good point," she said, moving closer to the gem.

As we moved closer to it, I was able to see the details better. It was about the size of my head and appeared to be nearly clear with a tint of blue. The gem was cut in angles that made it sparkle and shimmer as I moved alongside it.

Malin took up position on the opposite side of the gem from me. "Count of three?"

"One," I said, "two, three." I grabbed the gem with both hands.

Everything around us went black and I held my breath as I repressed a flicker of joy. I wasn't out of this yet. My hope was that this ended the second trial, but I had no idea where we'd end up.

I landed on my feet but hit the ground so hard I lost balance, falling to the side in a crumpled heap. Before I could take in my surroundings, I looked up to see if Malin had made it through.

She was across from me, also in a heap on the ground. She was laughing and the gem was nowhere to be seen.

I started laughing, too. The whole things seemed so ridiculous now that we were away from the woods. Catching my breath, I looked around and realized I wasn't back in the dungeon cell I'd started from. Polished wood floors, bookshelves that spanned the entire wall and a massive staircase greeted me. I knew this place. Flutters filled my chest as I pushed myself to standing, all traces of laughter gone. I was back at the Winter Palace.

Three guards rushed into the room, swords drawn. Malin yelped behind me and I put my hands up. "It's me," I said. "Cassia. She's with me. She's a friend."

Another figure emerged from behind the guards. He was dressed in a uniform complete with leather armor. A sword in his hand. Tristan looked ready for battle, but that didn't stop me from running right to him.

I stopped a hands breath away from him, lower lip trembling. He was here and he was safe.

"I heard you calling me, Cassia," Tristan said. "How did you..."

"The second trial pulled me away and delivered me here when I finished," I said. "Your father has one of the council members. I think she might have rigged my trial to bring me back here."

The tightness in Tristan's expression melted away as his blue eyes stared into mine. "I thought I'd lost you."

"I'm here. I'm safe." I didn't know how to react to him. Part of me wanted to burrow my face in his chest so I could feel his strong arms wrap around me. Part of me wanted to run my fingers through his hair and pull his mouth next to mine. But there was hesitation deep within that kept me standing still, unmoving, so close to him that I could feel his warmth.

"Your Grace," one of the guards said. "It's time. The soldiers are waiting for you."

"Soldiers?" I asked.

"We were going to wait until after Queen's Trial, but once my father took you, I called in my allies. Even the humans were willing to join in once they knew he'd taken you."

I felt like the air was leaving my chest. I'd just returned and I was starting to thread together my feelings for Tristan only to have him leave for battle. I opened my mouth to ask him to stay. To beg him not to go. But my voice came out steady and stronger than I expected. "Be careful. He has a member of the council, Jaya. She helped me get of there. And Nani's still there. Please get them out safely." I paused, forcing back the urge to ask him to stay here. For him to send the others and save himself. "Please be careful. I'd like you back. In one piece."

A half smile formed on Tristan's lips. "I've been waiting a long time to hear something like that from you."

"I mean it," I said.

"I'll come to you as soon as it's done. But you need to go somewhere safe," he said.

"She can stay with me," Malin said from behind me.

Tristan's brow furrowed as he took in the female behind me as if noticing her for the first time.

"Malin Valoi, Your Grace." Malin bobbed into a curtsy.

"Can you take her to the Spring Prince?" Tristan asked.

"Yes," she said.

"Cassia, there's so much I have to tell you, but it has to wait. Go now. I'll come for you as soon as I can." Tristan's expression hardened once more, the look of a male about to face his enemies.

Then, he turned away from me and walked down the hall, his guards behind him.

An empty echo filled my chest as I watched him walk away and at that moment, I knew Nani's guess was correct. Tristan and I shared a mating bond.

Chapter Twenty-One

✤

Malin's hands were on mine before I could think about what to do next. My stomach twisted as I felt the ground vanish from under me once again. Breathless, I ignored the wetness of my cheeks as we slid to wherever Malin was taking us. I should have been worried, but Malin caused me no ill feelings. I'd known her for mere hours, but I trusted her. I knew I should be suspicious of new people, but I couldn't bring myself to attach any of those feelings to her. I hoped my intuition wasn't failing me and I squeezed her hand tighter as we rushed through the void.

My feet touched down on soft earth and damp blades of grass brushed against my ankles. I took a deep breath, the scent of honeysuckle filling my nostrils. It was intoxicating and calming. Birds chipped overhead and a warm breeze rustled the leaves of the nearby trees. A sense of peace caressed me like a warm blanket.

Behind us, I saw a beautiful, sprawling home that looked like it belonged in a fairy tale. It was made of brown bricks and trimmed in dark brown wood. Each of the windows was bordered with shutters and all of the windows on the first floor had window boxes overflowing with blooming red and yellow flowers.

"Welcome to the Spring Court," Malin said.

I turned to her. "Thank you."

"I know you're not Queen yet," she said. "But I'm going to pretend you've already won. I've met most of the other candidates. Any one of them would have left me to die if they didn't kill me off upon meeting me in those woods. You're the exact thing we need in Faerie. It's been hard around here since the Winter Court broke off. And clearly, you seem to have some serious pull with the Winter Prince."

My cheeks heated. I knew she was right. As much as Tristan drove me crazy, I knew his affection for me was at the forefront of his decisions. I frowned, wondering why he'd spent so much time pushing me away if he felt the mating bond. Or did he not know it yet?

"I'm sorry about your prince," she said.

"I wouldn't say he's mine," I said, knowing the words were false. I was part of Tristan just as he was part of me. Just as I was connected to the other three princes, I needed Tristan in the same way. I knew it was going to cause complications, but I would have to deal with that later.

She smirked. "Alright."

"The Spring Prince, however, is mine." Just thinking of Ethan was making me feel safer than I had in days. "Can you take us to his home?"

She pointed. "This is his home. Charming, isn't it? He doesn't live with his father in the palace."

I hugged Malin. How someone who had known me for such a short time could anticipate my needs so well was beyond me. I was just grateful I found her.

Malin hugged me back and then the two of us stepped away from each other. I smiled at her. "Come with me."

She followed me to the doorway and stood behind me as I knocked. My knees went weak as Ethan answered and I wobbled on my feet.

Ethan caught me in his strong arms. "Cassia, is everything alright?"

"Yes, no," I said. "I'm not sure."

"Malin," Ethan said. "What's going on? Are your parents well?"

"They're fine," she said. "Cassia and I met during the second trial. The Winter Prince asked me to bring her here for safety."

"Come in," Ethan said. "I want to hear everything."

The three of us walked into the entryway and followed Ethan into a modestly appointed sitting room. Wood rocking chairs, a couch and two chairs with cushions over them formed a semi-circle around a fireplace.

Ethan guided me to the couch and I sat down. He took the seat next to me and Malin sat in one of the rocking chairs.

"I don't understand," Ethan said. "Did Tristan let you out of the favor?"

"Things got complicated." I played with a hole in the fabric of my dress. "I completed the first trial, then the Winter King took me. I would still be there if the second trial hadn't caused me to slide into the middle of a forest. Malin and I met each other there and we worked together to complete the task. When I was finished, it brought us back to Tristan's palace instead of to the Winter King. Tristan has amassed an army and is on his way to take down his father as we speak."

Ethan was silent, seeming to mull over everything I had just said. I condensed a lot of information into a few sentences and I watched him closely, waiting for him to speak.

Finally, he reached his hand over to me and clasped my fingers in his. "This war has been brewing for a long time. Tristan was bound to go after his father eventually. That has nothing to do with you. You're a catalyst to force his hand after years of him biding his time. As for the rest of it, we need to let the Council know where you are. The rules of Queens Trial are harsh. I'm afraid kidnapping isn't enough to grant your reprieve if you miss or are late to one of the tasks." He turned to Malin. "Thank you for bringing her to me. Have you been staying with your family?"

Malin nodded. "Yes. And I'm sure they're expecting me. May I borrow a horse?"

"I'll walk you out to the stables." Ethan turned to look at me. "Stay here. I'll be back in a few minutes."

I leaned back against the seat and closed my eyes. I brushed my hair off of my face and rested my hands on top of my head. Ethan's home, was quiet and smelled like flowers in a spring breeze. It had been a long time since I sat in silence someplace where I felt comfortable. The Winter palace had never felt safe to me, even though I knew Tristan wouldn't hurt me.

Tristan made me feel both heat and ice at the same. It was a burning intense emotion that I had come to associate with the Winter Prince. I thought it was driven by my dislike of him, but now that I thought about it, there was too much appeal to the feeling for me to walk away from it. There was a dangerous excitement to being around Tristan that I craved.

Ethan made me feel different. He was comfort and coziness and peace. Ethan made me feel like I was home. I knew I wouldn't be able to spend too much time away from him without feeling emptiness.

Then there was Dane, who was heat and fun and the promise of adventure. I smiled just thinking about him. Finally, I recalled Cormac's touch, the heat of him and the way he made me feel so safe as I gave up all control. Each of the princes was a piece of me and I needed them all. Right now, the comfort Ethan could bring was exactly what I needed. Had Tristan known that?

I lowered my hands to my lap and opened my eyes. I knew I needed to try and keep my focus on the trials not on juggling the whims of my heart. I wasn't even sure I had passed the second trial and if I had, I still had the third to worry about before I would have to go to the Queens Palace for the second part of the trials. There was still so much uncertainty ahead of me.

I heard the sound of the door opening and turned to see Ethan walking back into the house. He closed the door behind him and bolted it. "You should be safe here until we can figure out what to do next. You're lucky you ran in to Malin. I've known her most of her life, her family owns the farm and the lands that border my own. They're one of the few families in the Spring Court I would trust with my life." Ethan crossed the room to a small writing desk and pulled out a piece of paper and a pen. He scribbled across the paper then folded it up. Then he dropped the paper into a hole on the side of his desk and it vanished from sight.

"Is that for the council?" I asked, not even attempting to understand the magic he used to make the paper vanish.

"Yes. I let them know you're here so they can decide if you can compete from here or if they want you to move somewhere else." Ethan walked back over to the couch and sat so close to me our legs were touching.

He rested his large hand on my cheek and I leaned into his touch. Then, he slid his hand down to my chin and gently tilted my chin up so our eyes met. "I've been so worried. You have no idea how much I worried about you. I thought I was going to have to wait weeks to see you. I know I should feel terrible about all that you've been through but right now all I can think about is the fact that it brought you back to me sooner."

With his words, I felt my anxiety and worry melting away. With the danger surrounding us, I knew I should be grateful for any amount of time I got to spend where I felt safe and happy. I smiled at Ethan. "I'm not planning on going anywhere unless they drag me away from you."

Ethan leaned down and gently pressed his lips against mine.

He moved his mouth slowly and wove his fingers through my hair as he pulled me in deeper. My mind went blank, driving all my worries away as my hands took on a life of their own, exploring Ethan's body as he pressed into me.

Chapter Twenty-Two

❧❦❧

E arly morning sunshine streamed in through the sheer curtains in Ethan's room. I was laying on his chest, his arm around me. His warmth had kept me feeling safe and comfortable all night. Sunlight poured across Ethan's bare chest making every ripple of muscles look even more spectacular than they had in the candlelight last night. I didn't want to move from this bed, but I knew the third trial was going to come today.

Carefully, I turned in his arm, trying to wiggle my way out without disturbing him. Another arm closed in around me, pulling me closer to him. My bare breasts pressed against his chest and he let out a low growl.

His eyes were still closed as he lowered his face into the crook of my neck nuzzling me with his nose. I giggled. He brushed his soft lips against the sensitive skin of my neck, kissing me in a line all the way to my shoulder.

"You know we have things to do today," I said, instantly regretting the words.

He smiled lazily. "We do. But this is the first time you're waking with me in my bed in my home. It's hard to imagine letting you leave it now that I've had you here."

I sighed. "I feel the same way."

He kissed my forehead and released me from his embrace. I stood, walking away from the bed to where I had shed my clothes.

"I'm never going to get used to sharing you," Ethan said.

I froze, my back to him. My first thoughts going to Tristan and wondering how Ethan knew.

"Cormac and Dane are going to kill me if I keep you here without telling them you're here and safe," he said.

I let myself relax and arranged a smile on my face before turning back to him. "It would be the fair thing to do."

Ethan took a deep breath. "I have always considered myself fair, but I have to admit, I have to fight the urge to keep you to myself from time to time."

He let out a low growl and jumped from the bed, grabbing me and playfully carrying me back. "One more round before I announce to the others that you've returned to us."

I shrieked as Ethan threw me on the bed. He kissed my cheeks, my chin, my neck, down to my collarbone, then kept kissing me. Laughing, I surrendered to his kisses.

A knock on the door interrupted us just as Ethan's fingers had slipped between my thighs. I grabbed a blanket and covered myself and Ethan hopped down from the bed, striding over to the door unconcerned by the fact that he was completely naked.

I watched the muscles on his back ripple and the tightening of his butt and thighs as he walked. For a moment, I wondered how I'd gotten so lucky. How was it that I was here with this beautiful male?

Ethan paused at the door, grabbing a sword that was propped against the wall. I hadn't noticed it before and it made me wonder if there were more weapons hiding around his house. I needed to be more observant. In the sleepy comfort of Ethan's embrace I had stopped worrying about my safety. As he gripped the sword in his hand, alertness snapped back into place and all of the contentment I had felt melted away. I gripped the bedding in my hands tighter, wishing I had a weapon nearby. Instinctively, I felt for my magic and it rose up to greet me with a familiar tingling sensation. I still didn't know what I'd do with it if I needed to, but knowing it was there and knowing that I could make things happen made me feel more confident.

Ethan opened the door quickly, lifting the sword to a defensive position at the same time.

"Put away your weapon," Cormac said without pause. His eyes moved past Ethan to where I sat on the bed, covering my naked body with blankets.

I swallowed as heat rose to my cheeks as embarrassment swirled inside me. I'd never hidden my relationship with the princes from the others, but I didn't expect to have one of them walk in on me with another. How must he be feeling? Would he be hurt or feel betrayed that I was here with Ethan and not with him? We hadn't even told him yet that I returned.

Cormac's lips parted and his eyes softened. A small smile played on his lips as he walked right past Ethan to me.

He either didn't notice or didn't care that I was naked in Ethan's bed. Cormac swept me up in his arms, lifting me off the bed in an embrace that took my breath away. He buried his face in my hair, warm breath against my ear. "I'm so grateful you're safe."

All the awkwardness of being in Ethan's room vanished. I let go of the blanket and wrapped my arms around his neck, breathing in the scent of him. Tears blurred my vision and I blinked them away. Cormac let me go and helped tuck the blanket up around me.

"Dane is well," Cormac said, as if realizing I'd want an update. "I was sent at the Queen's behest. She's requested your return to court. Something terrible has happened."

Ethan walked over to us, my dress in his hands. He'd pulled on a pair of trousers and a loose fitting tunic that was open in the front revealing most of his chest. I clenched my thighs together, feeling a surge of heat between my legs that had been stirred by our interrupted moving interlude.

Ethan handed me my clothes, then turned back to Cormac. "What is it?"

I tugged the tunic over my head, then stood to pull the skirt over my hips. "What happened?"

"The trial has been compromised," Cormac said. "Several of the candidates were given false trials and they didn't survive."

"What do you mean by *false trials*?" I asked.

"The last trial had a travel enchantment," Cormac said to Ethan.

"Cassia told me about it," Ethan said.

"Of course," Cormac said. "She was fortunate. Several of the messages were altered and the candidates were sent elsewhere."

My stomach twisted into knots and I backed up to the bed, sitting down as numbness worked its way from my chest down my arms and into my fingers. My mouth wasn't working as the conclusion formed in my mind. It was sabotage. And I knew it was aimed at me.

"We're not sure who got to the letters, but we think they intended to change all of them and were interrupted," he said. "It's pure luck that Cassia got one of the correct letters."

I shook my head as I forced myself to push back against the numbness. I wasn't helpless, I needed to say something, fight against this. I knew this was my fault. "Someone wanted me dead bad enough to endanger all of the candidates."

Cormac was silent, but I watched as his temples bulged when he tightened his jaw.

"How many?" I asked, my voice small.

"There are only four of you left," he said.

A chill ran down my spine. Only four of the letters had been left untouched. "All the candidates who received the false letters were killed?"

Cormac nodded. "They were sent directly in front of a tear to the Under. They never stood a chance."

"Tiana," I said. "It was Tiana. She probably knew her way into wherever they kept the letters. She's working with the Under. She wants me dead."

I had hoped she didn't want me dead bad enough to sacrifice all the candidates for the trial, but I was wrong.

"I believe she's the culprit," Cormac said. "The Queen doesn't want to believe it, but I think she's coming around to the idea."

"What happens if the candidates are all killed?" I asked. "Who then becomes Queen?"

"That's never happened before," Ethan said. "I'm not even sure of what the rules dictate in that situation."

"I wondered the same thing," Cormac said. "I asked the Council the same question."

"And?" I asked, holding my breath as I waited for an answer.

"The Queen's next of kin gains the crown until a new Trial can be organized," Cormac said.

Ethan blew out a breath. "And only a Queen can call for a Trial. If Tiana gets the crown on her head, she's not taking it off."

"We can't let that happen," I said.

"I know. That's what I need you for, Ethan. We are going to find Tiana and stop her before she can do any more damage." He held up a scroll and unrolled it.

I noticed the wax seal on the bottom of the paper and then read the words. It was a declaration of authority for Cormac, giving him permission to serve as executioner if he captured Tiana.

My throat tightened. I knew Cormac was often given the task of hunting monsters, but Tiana was something worse. Not only was she a monster, she could control the monsters.

"You can't go," I said. "Have them send someone else."

"You know we have to go after her," Cormac said. "She's not going to stop until she kills you and we swore to protect you."

My brow furrowed and I scrambled to think of anything that might keep them here with me, but I knew nothing was going to convince them to stay. "Then I'm going with you. I can help."

"No," Cormac said. "They have determined to run the last trial. You have to finish this or all those other candidates died for nothing."

Chapter Twenty-Three

※❖※

Cormac reached into his tunic and pulled out a small envelope with my name scrawled across the front in large, curving letters. "After you pass the last trial, you can return to the Autumn Court. As long as you pass, you're in the final four since there are only four of you left. You're nearly there. Once you're back at the Autumn Court, we can protect you better. Dane's waiting for you there."

I took the letter from him and stared at the wax seal holding the envelope closed. What could they possibly ask of me now? There was so much danger. So many terrible things. Tears in the Under, Tianna openly opposing the throne, all the candidates dead without a chance to experience the rest of their lives. How could they possibly want this to continue in the midst of everything else? I took a deep breath, knowing that things were different for the Fae. They didn't cry over a little bloodshed the way humans did. For all I knew this sort of thing happened every time Queen's Trial happened.

I could feel Cormac and Ethan's gaze upon me as I stared down at the final trial. I traced my fingers over the wax as I gathered my strength. I had to do this. I had to prove myself worthy even if most of the competition had been eliminated. Becoming Queen wasn't what I had set out to do, but when the alternative was Tiana, what choice did I have?

I looked up at the princes. "I suppose I might as well get started."

I slid my finger under the seal under the wax to break the seal but Cormac's hand came down on top of mine. "We can't be here for this one. You had help on the first two, the final trial must be completed by you alone."

He looked over at Ethan. "We are to return to the palace and begin the search for Tiana. The Queen has requests for help immediately."

Ethan's brow furrowed. "That leaves her unguarded."

"I don't like it either," Cormac said. "But I don't want her to lose her chance to become Queen, do you?"

Ethan frowned, then nodded. "Be careful, Cassia. We'll meet you back at the Autumn Palace as soon as we can."

"Dane is already there," Cormac said. "They told me you'd end up there when you finished. When you get back, find Dane and don't leave his side."

I nodded. My throat felt dry as I watched them leave the room, giving me the privacy that was requested for me to complete the final trial. I wasn't sure I was ready, but I knew I had to do this. And the sooner I got it finished, the sooner I'd get to Dane where I would feel safe again.

Sasha's warning about my death during the trial echoed in the back of my mind. But I couldn't focus on that now. Once I returned to the Autumn Palace, maybe Dane could take me to his home to wait for the next stage of the Trials. Unless that was the part I was to die in. I shook my head, realizing that there was a reason why Tristan had kept some things from me. Worrying about what was to come wasn't going to help me survive right now.

There wasn't much of a choice. Before I could lose my nerve,

I broke the wax seal off of the envelope and opened the letter. Before I even got to read the contents, I was pulled away, sliding through the void wherever the third trial was. I tried to steady myself, taking calming breaths. I'd expected it this time, but it was still just as startling as the first time I slid. As the darkness closed in on me I reminded myself that all I had to do was pass this trial and I was in the next round.

I needed to do this and I needed to do it well. And this time, I knew I couldn't ask for help from anyone or offer to work together if I happened to run into one of the other remaining candidates. This had to be all me. I'd had a feeling I was going to be forced to work alone at some point, but I still didn't like the idea of being so isolated.

As my feet touched down, I managed to maintain my balance as the darkness faded from my vision. I blinked, expecting sunlight, but there wasn't any. I could hardly see in front of me at all. Shivering once again, I wished I would've thought to grab a cloak or something to keep myself warm before I opened the envelope.

It had been morning when I left Ethan's, but wherever I was, it was no longer daytime. The moon shone down from the sky illuminating icy snow under my feet. I took slow careful steps, and managed to stay on top of the crusted snow without falling through. It was more like ice at this point and I wondered exactly where I was.

The snow wasn't fresh, it had been there a while, likely thawed and refrozen several times to create this type of surface. Sparse trees scattered across the landscape offered little in the way of cover if anything attacked. Moving forward and getting this over with was my only option.

Thankful for the light of the moon and the snow underfoot to help everything look brighter, I hesitantly moved forward, testing each step before I put my full weight on my foot. Once when we were children, Rose had stepped on what she thought was just snow, but it turned out it was covering a rather large puddle. When she stepped on the surface, she broke through the snow and the ice underneath, falling into the small pit. Thankfully, the water only went up to her mid-calf and it wasn't anything she could drown in.

I still remembered the look of surprise on her face and the pain she was in from the contact of the cold water on her skin. Her screams were so loud that I was terrified she was going to die. She recovered with dry clothes and a warm blanket by the fire but for a few minutes, I was worried I was going to lose her. All because we didn't watch where we put our feet.

I didn't know where I was or what was under the packed snow and I couldn't afford to make any mistakes. My movement was cautious and slow. I did my best to keep my steps silent, but the sound of crunching snow still caught me off guard every few steps. Each sound seemed to echo through the expense of landscape around me, alerting anything or anyone that was nearby of my presence.

I stopped walking and took a few deep breaths. I needed to figure out what my task was so I could create a plan. I wished I'd had a chance to read the letter.

I CLOSE my eyes for second and felt for my magic, hoping that if there were something magical nearby I might be able to detect it the way I had in the last trial. My heart jumped as I felt the familiar pulse rise up to greet me. Something outside of me was sending a magical signature similar to mine.

Hope flickered inside me, intermingling with desperation. I moved closer to the sense of magic, hoping whatever it was, it was the thing I was supposed to find or do to complete the trial. I had a feeling it wasn't going to be as easy as the last two. I'd shown I could ask for help and shown that I could detect magic. This trial would probably require that I use magic. My stomach twisted in anticipation as I crept closer to the source. I still had no training on how to use magic. I hadn't had a chance to talk to Tristan about any of it. All I had to do was pass this trial, but what if I couldn't do it?

Thoughts of Tristan clouded my focus, momentarily making me forget the weight of the trial at hand. He was dealing with a war right now and all I had to do was get through some silly test. It made what I was doing seem unimportant and foolish. I should be helping him, but I got so swept up in my reunion with Ethan that I didn't consider how much danger he was in. Was he safe? Had he already completed his fight? Had he rescued Nani and Jaya?

I wondered if I would feel a sense of danger or pain if he was injured. I hadn't felt any major disruptions that made me fear for Tristan's safety. Hopefully that meant everything was going well. We shared a mating bond and even though I hadn't had a chance to discuss it with him, I think he knew it too. Was that the big thing he'd been keeping from me? Why did he do that? Was he hoping I'd come up with it on my own or that it would go away?

I shook my head, refocusing on the trial. I knew I couldn't lose sight of my purpose. The sooner I figured this out, the sooner I'd return. Then, I could find out what was going on with Tristan and with Tiana and with everything else that seemed to be falling apart.

In the distance, a green light started to flicker, pulsing in time to the magic that was flowing through my veins. Whatever it was it seemed to be calling to me. I picked up my pace, not as cautious as I had been, hoping I wouldn't encounter any surprises between now and the time that I reached the green light.

I reached the light sooner than anticipated, the lack of challenges on my route was making me feel uncomfortable. Unease weighed heavily on me as I approached what appeared to be a green lantern suspended in the air.

This couldn't be it; it couldn't be this easy. Granted, the lantern was several body lengths above me, making it difficult to reach. Was that the goal? If I retrieved the lantern, would the trial be complete?

I stared at the light, breathing in time with its pulse as I contemplated how I could reach it. Behind me, someone laughed. A horrible crackling sound that made my skin crawl. Feeling chilled to the bone, I turned to see who could possibly be standing behind me making that kind of noise. Tiana was still laughing when my gaze met hers.

Chapter Twenty-Four

⁂

Tiana didn't laugh long. Before I could fully grasp what was happening, she charged me, wrapping her arms around me and knocking me to the ground. She stood quickly, slamming her foot on top of my chest, pinning me in place. I heard something crack and sharp pain splintered through me. I screamed as my vision blurred, the pain threatening to take away my consciousness.

Gasping for breath, I struggled to roll away from her, grabbing her foot and lifting it so she landed on the ground next to me. On all fours she sneered at me, showing pointed teeth. "No one's coming to save you this time."

I pushed myself to standing and backed away from her. She shouldn't be here. Ethan and Cormac were trying to find her and the council had been made aware of her plan. Surly, she couldn't alter the trials twice?

Realization made my eyes widen. Somehow she had tricked Cormac into coming for me. "You sent Cormac."

"I was Cormac," she said, shifting into the familiar form of the Autumn Prince before my eyes. "You need to learn to be more aware of your surroundings." The words came out in Cormac's voice, not hers. But now that I was aware of her trick, I could tell there was something that wasn't quite right. I should have noticed before.

My nostrils flared and I clenched my teeth, furious at her deception. "What did you do with him. And what did you do with Ethan?"

Last I'd seen them, they were leaving me alone in Ethan's house.

She melted back into herself. "Cormac doesn't even know you're here. Nobody does. As far as they know, you're tucked away in the Winter Court."

"What did you do with Ethan?" I repeated.

"He'll wake soon," she said. "Not soon enough to save you, but he'll live."

"If you hurt him..." The threat hung between us, empty words that I wasn't even sure I could deliver.

"You really should be worrying about yourself right now," she said.

My magic roared to life, clawing at my insides, desperate for release. I had to defeat Tiana. I had to save myself, find Ethan, and keep her from ever hurting anyone again.

Tiana smiled, a wicked grin. "I can feel your magic. So you want to play, do you?"

Behind Tiana the green lantern pulsed above her, then it started to crackle and sputter. I took my eyes off of my opponent to look up. Green sparks shot out from the lantern, small at first, then growing larger until some of them reached down to the ground below like sickening green lightning.

Tiana laughed again and I tore my gaze from the light back to her.

"You are such a fool," Tiana said. "Even if you knew how to use your magic, you still wouldn't stand a chance. In just a moment my creatures will come, you can't stop us. You can't stop me."

"You can't possibly think anything is worth letting those creatures into this world," I said. Desperate for any kind of distraction as I channeled all of my magic to my hands. I still wasn't sure what I was going to do, but I let instinct take over, sending my magic to a point of contact so I could release it at her.

"Oh but it is, because I won't just rule this world, I will also rule the Under," she said.

My heart thundered in my chest as magic sent heat through my veins until it burned in my palms. I wanted to take Tiana down more than ever.

Whatever was coursing through me was hot and dangerous and I knew it was my best chance. I released the magic, turning my palms out toward Tiana pushing everything I had in her direction.

The magic came out white-hot. My hair stuck to my sweaty forehead and I felt beads of perspiration slide down my back. Exhaustion began to set in as I sent the glowing light current toward her. It was more intense than the usual white light I sent out. This was hotter and instead of hanging in the air blinding us, it traveled in a stream of concentrated light that was aimed right at Tiana.

Finally, breathing heavy, I relinquished the magic. My arms dropped to my side and my shoulder sank. Whatever I had done had taken most of my strength. In front of me smoke rose from the ground and I hoped whatever I had done was enough. As the smoke began to clear my heart sank. In front of me, seemingly unharmed, was Tiana.

"Still trying to depend on your light magic," she clicked her tongue. "I was hoping to see you come up with something new."

I was too tired to speak and I knew I needed to save my strength so I glared at her with the most defiance I could muster. Behind her, the lantern sputtered and the green light faded. The moon once again our only source of light. My breath came in clouds, the cold of the night returned in full force now that the light was gone.

Whatever horrible magic she had created to lure me in seemed to be gone. I wondered what she would throw at me next. I knew Tiana wouldn't play by the rules, if there were any rules in magic.

I balled my hands into fists, preparing to hit her if she got too close to me. Without some time for my magic to recharge, it was all I had. It wasn't much, but at least I could go down trying to defend myself.

A screeching sound punctuated the empty landscape, vibrating so hard that I could feel it in my bones. Then, the sound of something ripping echoed through the night. It was as if a huge piece of fabric had been pulled apart.

Just beyond Tiana I saw the sky begin to split. It was as if it were tearing open. Where there had been starry sky and moonlight I could see smoke pouring out into our world from an opening that hadn't been there before.

That must have been what the lantern was for. Tiana created a tear to the Under. How many of these had she made? How many of these would she continue to make? How could she do this to Faerie? Jaw clenched, I looked back at Tiana. "You are a monster. You belong in the Under with all of the rest of them."

"You were raised in the human world. So you know better than anyone that we're all monsters here. Capable of terrible things. That's all this world is. A realm of monsters. The only difference between us and the creatures of the Under is our magic."

Growling came from the tear. I tensed, terrified to find out what Tiana had released on me. I took a few unsteady steps backward, seeking more distance between myself and the creatures.

My magic simmered below the surface, springing back to life without warning. It tugged and pulled as if it wanted me to go closer to the tear. That didn't make any sense. I knew how dangerous the creatures that lived in the Under were and I knew how much harm they could cause. Yet, the opening seemed to call to me.

"Come on out, darlings." Tiana was facing the tear, ignoring me.

My nostrils flared as I glared at her. She didn't see me as a threat and she wasn't going to take me down herself. She was waiting for something to come and finish me off. "You're a coward."

She turned to look at me, one eyebrow raised. "What was that?"

"You are a coward. You're sneaky and manipulative and you're taking the throne in a cowardly way."

Her upper lip curled as she bared her teeth. "You don't know what you're taking about. You aren't even a real Fae. You should have stayed in the human realm where you belong."

"Then face me yourself. Why let the monsters do the deed for you? Are you such a coward that you can't even take down a nearly human girl on your own?" I knew the words were dangerous. I was playing with fire. But as I stood there, watching her face contort as she considered my insults, I felt my magic growing.

Chapter Twenty-Five

Yellow eyes flashed at the tear, growling low and guttural. The sound set my nerves on edge, but I couldn't back down. Whatever was coming through from the Under couldn't be any worse than Tiana.

Again, magic tugged at me, drawing me nearer to the tear. I ignored the pull and focused on the Fae in front of me. She waited, hands at her sides, as if calling to the monsters that were emerging behind her.

For a second, I focused on the movement behind her, catching my first full glimpse at the creatures she'd summoned. My heart pounded harder as my gaze fixed on a massive wolf. The creature was three times the size of a wolf in the human realm, its ears nearly the size of my head. The beast pulled back its lips, snarling in my direction. Sharp canines dripped with saliva as the monster growled again.

"Get her," Tiana called.

"No," I said on reflex. "I'm not going to harm you."

The wolf's ears flattened against its head, its black fur standing on edge, raised almost like a mane around its sharp face.

"I summoned you, beast," Tiana said. "You belong to me."

"No," I said again. "You are your own creature. You belong to no one. You don't have to listen to her. This isn't your fight."

My magic flared as I spoke, shooting through me as if I'd lit an inner flame.

The wolf took a few steps away from the tear, walking slowly toward Tiana. I swallowed down my fear and felt for the thread that connected me to the magic inside me. I focused on holding onto the feeling, keeping my magic simmering below the surface, ready for me to grab hold of it if needed. I didn't want to hurt the creature if it wasn't trying to hurt me. The monster Tiana had summoned wasn't a poisonous Sodalis, it was too similar to the wolves that prowled the woods in the human world. I knew the wolves were dangerous only when provoked. I didn't intend to provoke it.

"Kill her," Tiana said through clenched teeth. Her frustration was obvious as she pointed to me while turning to look at the wolf. "Do it now."

I kept my hands at my sides and spread my fingers wide, trying to show that I was holding no weapons. "I don't intend harm."

"I am your mistress," Tiana said, desperation seeping into her voice.

"Send the creature home," I said. "This isn't her fight. It's between us. Why bring her into it?"

"The creature is a servant," Tiana said. "Like all lesser creatures, it must be told what to do."

The wolf snarled, turning toward Tiana, haunches ruffled in irritation.

"Animals are not here to serve us," I said. "Send her home. Close up the tear. Then face me yourself, you coward."

I took a step closer to Tiana, ignoring the wolf. I knew she wouldn't attack me now. I could feel her emotions intermingling with mine. She seemed to instinctively know how to draw the magic out of me, connecting us in a way that I couldn't explain.

Whatever it was, I knew I was safe from the wolf. The only real danger here was from Tiana.

"You need to stop this," I said. "Turn yourself in to the Queen. End this now."

"You don't get to choose how this goes," she said. "And you certainly don't get to command me. You shouldn't even exist."

She pulled a dagger from somewhere in the folds of her dress and charged me. I dove to the side to avoid the weapon and landed in a heap on the hard snow. Pushing myself up, I extended my hands out in front of me, prepared to disarm her as best I could.

Before I could make a move, the wolf leaped into the air, coming down on Tiana in a blur of fur and a flash of teeth and claws. The wolf growled. Tiana screamed.

My pulse raced and my eyes widened. A surge of power raced through me, intense and overwhelming. I cried out as I felt the rush of the fight, the energy of the attack, the feel of the kill.

When the wolf bit down on Tiana's throat, I could taste the coppery blood as if I'd bitten down on her myself.

Tiana grunted then there was only silence.

The wolf left a trail of bloody paw prints across the frozen snow as she padded away from her kill.

Tiana lay on the frozen ground, unmoving. A slow moving stream of crimson blood spread from her body like a river of death. I could smell the blood sticking to damp fur as if it were on me. I looked down at my hands but all that was there was scrapes from where I'd hit the ground.

I looked over at the wolf. She was licking her bloody paws.

I sank to my knees, exhausted as the connection between myself and the wolf shattered. Somehow, the creature and I had formed an alliance that went beyond the loyalty of a typical human or Fae bond with an animal. I had felt like I was inside the wolf, feeling what she felt. And she knew the threat that Tiana was to me. She'd read my emotions and protected me.

Slowly, I lifted a shaky hand into the air, extending it toward the wolf as a peace offering between the two of us. Whatever magic I had tapped into was long gone so I wasn't sure what would happen. I was too grateful for her help to walk away without showing her how much I appreciated her.

The wolf stopped licking her paw and turned to look at me. Her ears went back again and she sniffed the air. Then, she walked over to me, her claws making clicking sounds on the frozen earth.

She stopped in front of my outstretched fingers and sniffed my hand.

"Thank you," I said.

She took a few steps closer to me and I cautiously placed my hand on her neck, gently patting her. "Thank you."

The wolf leaned in to my touch then sat on the ground. I laughed. She was just a like a larger version of a dog someone might keep as a pet. I scooted a little closer and scratched her behind her ears. "I guess there are some wonderful things that can come from the Under. Just like there are some terrible things that can come from here."

With a sigh, I lowered my hand and looked at the tear that was still sitting open. I had a feeling whatever came through there next might not be as sweet as the wolf. I couldn't stay here.

With a grunt, I pushed myself to standing and turned to walk away from the tear. I didn't know how to slide and I had no idea where I was. I had no choice, I had to call to Ethan.

The sound of claws on snow trailed behind me and I turned to see the wolf was staying behind me. "Are you coming with me, then?"

She caught up to me and kept pace next to my side. I reached over and patted her head. "Alright, then."

Having the wolf by my side made me feel safer as I walked away from the tear. Silently, I called out to Ethan, hoping he would find me soon.

Chapter Twenty-Six

Ethan wasn't alone when he found me. Dane crashed into me, lifting me off of my feet as he pulled me close.

The wolf next to me growled. I pushed away from Dane and turned to her. "It's okay, these are my friends."

Ethan set his hands on either side of my face. "Are you hurt?"

I shook my head. "I'm alright."

"Cormac's not even at the palace," Ethan said. "He was sent to take care of a tear. Whoever came to get me wasn't Cormac. We came as soon as we could."

"It was Tiana," I said, gesturing behind me. "And she left a tear open."

"Is that where your new friend came from?" Dane asked, eyeing the wolf suspiciously.

"She saved my life. I was no match for Tiana," I said.

"Where is she now?" Ethan asked.

"Dead. Near the tear she opened," I said.

"Get her somewhere safe, Dane," Ethan said. "I'll take care of the tear."

"We'll be at my place," Dane said. "She can contact the

council from there. If Tiana managed to infiltrate the Autumn Palace I don't trust their security."

"Tiana knew every detail about that place, I'm sure it's safe," Ethan said.

"No," I said, remembering Sasha's words about my impending doom. "I don't want to go there. I want to go anywhere but there."

"Take her to the Academy," Ethan said. "At least it's neutral territory."

Dane offered his hand. "Come on, let's get you somewhere warm."

The wolf whined, looking up at me with pleading eyes.

"Don't you want to go back to your family before Ethan closes the tear?" I asked her.

Sadness, deep and longing pooled in my gut as I looked into the creature's eyes. "You're alone."

She whined again, then pawed at the ground in front of me.

"Can we bring her?" I asked.

"I don't think we can slide with a wolf," Dane said.

"I can bring her with me, if she'll consent to allow it," Ethan said, inclining his head toward the wolf.

She cocked her head to the side as if considering the offer.

"You can trust him," I said. "He can bring you to me."

The wolf shook her head, her thick fur rustling. Then, she trotted over to Ethan and sat next to him.

I smiled at her. "I'll see you soon. Keep him safe for me, will you? He's important to me."

I wasn't sure how I'd connected with the wolf, but I knew she understood me. Feeling better about leaving Ethan now that he had some protection, I accepted Dane's hand. "You both better come back safe to me."

"We will," Ethan said, offering his hand to the wolf for her to sniff. She rubbed her head along his hand, accepting his offer of friendship.

Dane squeezed my hand and this time, when the blackness took hold, I let out a breath of relief, relishing the sensation. I was safe with Dane. I had finished the third trial and Tiana was dead. The risks on my life were winding down. Now, all I had to do was get through the next part and survive whatever it was that was supposed to cause my demise at the Autumn Palace. But that didn't matter right now. Right now, I was with Dane and I was going somewhere that wasn't part of Queen's Trial.

I squeezed Dane's hand tighter just as the darkness faded. Before I could adjust to the new surroundings, Dane had me in his arms again, pulling me down with him.

I landed on top of his firm chest and he rolled so I was on my side facing him, strong arms circled around me. I let myself sink into his embrace, and took in the warmth of the room we were in.

The two of us were on a small bed, barely large enough for someone Dane's size, let alone a partner. Gray blankets and white pillows completed the bed, showing no signs of the riches or luxury I'd grown used to in the Fae realm.

Not caring where we were, I nuzzled into Dane's chest and breathed in his clean, rosemary scent. My skin tingled as I adjusted to the warmth of the room and the male who still had me wrapped in his arms. I never wanted to leave. "Can we just lay like this forever?"

"I wish we could." He kissed the top of my head. "I was so worried about you."

I pulled away from him enough to look up into his eyes. "Thank you for coming to help me."

"Always," he said. "I just wish I'd left when I first felt your fear."

"What do you mean?" I asked.

"I'm not good with this kind of stuff," Dane said.

"What kind of stuff?" I asked.

"Love stuff," Dane said.

My cheeks heated. "You mean?"

"I knew you were special, Cassia," Dane said. "From the minute I first saw you, I wanted you. I just didn't realize it was going to be so different from the way I wanted other females. I can't stop thinking about you. Even after I had you. And trust me, that's not typical for me."

"Dane." I pulled one of my arms free and set my palm on his cheek.

"Honestly, I never thought I'd feel a mating connection to anyone, let alone a future Queen."

I opened my mouth to speak, but Dane moved too quickly, his lips on mine before I could respond. I moved into the kiss, forcing my feelings for him into the movement of my lips. My tongue found his and we explored each other as the kiss deepened.

Dane's hand moved behind my neck, his fingers tangling in my hair. Our bodies pressed tighter together and I could feel his hardness against my thigh.

His hand slid down my back to my hips before dipping up under my tunic. His bare hand on my skin sent a chill through me and I moaned into his mouth.

Dane pulled away from the kiss, a smile on his lips. "How did I get so lucky?"

I bit down on my swollen lip and stared back at him, breathless from our kiss. "I love you, Dane."

It didn't feel like enough to describe the bond that screamed between the two of us. The words felt inadequate, too human to express what the Fae mating bond was like. Alone here with Dane, I felt the intensity of our bond. It was just as strong as it was with the others, but what we had was different. He made me feel like everything was on fire and I wanted to lose myself to the heat.

I scooted out of his embrace, careful not to fall off the bed. With a smirk, I lifted my tunic over my head.

Dane's hands were on my breasts immediately, a strong,

calloused hand cupping each of them. He caressed them gently, then leaned forward and pulled the right nipple into his mouth, sucking on it until it came to a point. Then, he moved to the other nipple.

I moaned as arousal traveled lower, making my undergarments damp. I needed him.

Feeling brave, I loosened Dane's belt, then reached my hand down his trousers, finding his erection. Carefully, I moved my hand up and down the velvet skin, enjoying how it grew even larger at my touch.

Dane shuddered slightly, his hands frozen in place on my breasts as I distracted him with my touch. Seeming to regain his control, he lifted my hand away from his trousers before sliding them down his hips.

I reached for it again, but he stopped me. Before I could object, he was pulling my skirt down. I lifted my hips to help him remove the clothing. He finished undressing and the two of us stared at each other for a moment before he lifted me on top of him.

Dane was sitting on the bed and slowly, he lowered me on to his lap. I sat on my knees, his erection brushed against my soft folds. Gently, Dane guided me down so he could enter me slowly.

I gasped as the tip found its way inside me, then held my breath as he lowered me more. My insides stretched to accommodate him, filling me completely.

Dane guided my hips, lifting his until we found a rhythm. I moaned as the pleasure grew with each thrust. My chest was pressed against his and I wrapped my arms around his back, digging my fingers into his firm muscles as the pleasure escalated.

Hands still on my hips, Dane increased the speed. I gasped as little shockwaves rolled through me. He pressed his lips against mine, pulling me into a hungry kiss as the pressure mounted. I moaned into his mouth, then broke away from the kiss, tossing my head back as an explosion worked its way through my core. I screamed in release just as Dane finished.

Exhausted and content, I leaned forward, resting my forehead against Dane's chest. I could feel the thumping of his heart, our breaths in time with each other. Dane wrapped his arms around my back while I remained pressed against him. He was safety and strength and love. And I couldn't believe how lucky I was to have him.

Chapter Twenty-Seven

As much as I wanted to lay with Dane until I fell asleep, I knew we'd be interrupted soon enough. And for once, I wanted to be in my clothes when the knock at the door came.

Cormac arrived just after I laced up the borrowed boots Dane found for me. Dane held his hands out in front of him. "Hold on there."

Cormac frowned, but stopped.

I could feel the magic crackle in the air as Dane left his hands outstretched in front of the Autumn Prince. I shuddered as I recalled how the pretend Cormac had acted toward me. How had Tiana known to be so familiar with me? Had she been inside my head?

Dane dropped his hands, then moved closer to Cormac, clapping the prince on his back. "Welcome back, brother."

Cormac returned the friendly gesture, giving Dane an almost-hug before walking into the room. He stopped in front of me, throat bobbing as he swallowed.

He seemed unsure of himself. As if he was being shy. That wasn't like him at all. Brooding, closed off, sure, but shy was new.

"Cormac," I said, breaking the silence. "I'm so glad to see you."

"I'm sorry," he said. "I left the palace. I fell right into her trap. I understand if you want to eliminate me as consort."

I moved closer to Cormac and took his hand, clasping it in mine. "Of course I don't want to do that. I need you. This wasn't your fault."

"It was," he said. "I should have known the message requesting me was fake. I know better than that."

"She tricked all of us," I said. "She knew all of our weaknesses, but that's never going to happen again. She's gone. She can't hurt us anymore."

Cormac rubbed his thumb over my hand. "I won't let anyone harm you again. I swear I'll protect you better."

"And you'll have help," Dane said. "She's got all of us here."

"You can't all be with me all of the time," I said. "Sometimes, I'll need to protect myself. But you can all help me learn how to use my magic so I can defend myself better. I got lucky this time. But I can't rely on luck."

"How did you defeat Tiana?" Cormac asked. "Ethan didn't say. He was in a hurry when he arrived back at the Autumn Palace."

"I made friends with a wolf," I said.

Cormac smiled and brushed his thumb against my cheek. "I knew your Autumn magic was strong."

"It wasn't just any wolf," Dane added. "It was from the Under."

Cormac lifted an eyebrow. "That is a surprise."

"I've had enough surprises to last me a lifetime during these trials," I said. "I'm so glad the first part is over."

Cormac dropped his hand from my face and his expression darkened. "Not quite."

"What do you mean?" Dane asked.

"What is it, Cormac?" I asked.

"You never actually completed the third trial," he said. "The whole trial was falsified so it doesn't count."

"Okay," I said, trying to keep my disappointment in check. "So I take the third trial, then."

"It's not that simple," Cormac said. "They already ran the third trial. You missed it. Based on the rules, you're out."

"No," I said. "That's not fair. I didn't know it wasn't the third trial. They can't kick me out for that."

"I know," Cormac said. "I've already requested a meeting with the Council on your behalf. You'll have to appeal your case."

"What?" Heat rose in my chest. "They can't do this. I didn't do anything wrong."

"I know," Cormac said, again. "But you'll still have to speak with them. We'll try to make them understand."

I staggered back, bumping into the bed. I sat down and rested my head in my hands. After all I'd been through, I thought I was at least done with the first part of the trial. Now, it turns out I might not have anything to show for the last few days.

"Cassia," Cormac said. "I know you've been through a lot, but we need to go. They're waiting for us."

I dropped my hands and looked up. "Right now?"

"Don't worry, love," Dane said. "We'll go with you. We'll help them see sense."

Cormac gave Dane a look that was probably a warning. "You know we can't enter the chamber. She has to do this alone."

He turned back to me. "I have faith in you, Cassia. And we'll be right outside the doors waiting for you when you finish. No matter what they decide, we're not going anywhere, are we, Dane?"

"Giant wolves couldn't keep me away," Dane said with a grin.

Blowing out a long breath, I nodded. "Let's get this over with."

I PACED THE HALL, waiting for the council to summon me. They'd taken over the throne room at the Autumn Palace but the Queen was nowhere in sight. I knew she couldn't do anything on my behalf, but it would have been nice to at least see her.

"You can sit down, Cassia," Dane said as I walked past him again.

"I can't," I said, turning to walk the other direction again.

"Deep breaths," he said.

I glared at him.

"Or not," he said.

"Cassia," Cormac said, catching my arm. "You have to calm down. The council won't respond to emotions. You have to be honest and clear. You can't get upset or let them get to you. Do you understand?"

I swallowed hard, then nodded. I wasn't sure how I was supposed to remain calm, but I had to try.

"Cassia!"

I looked up to see Ethan running down the hall. He stopped in front of me and Cormac released my arm, giving the two of us some space.

"I'm so glad I caught you before you had to go in," he said.

I gave him a quick hug, overly aware of the other eyes on me. "Thank the gods you're safe. Did you get the tear sealed?"

"Yes," he said. "And your new friend is settled in an empty stable. She's terrifying the horses, but they'll get used to her. You should visit her when you're done. Take him with you," he said, pointing to Cormac.

"Thank you, Ethan," I said.

"Cassia?" an unfamiliar female voice called.

I turned to see the doors to the throne room open. A short, curvy female Fae with long red hair was watching me from the threshold.

"We're ready for you."

I inclined my head in what I hoped was a proper sign of respect then glanced back at my males.

Cormac lifted his eyebrows. "Go."

Ethan and Dane nodded.

I turned away from them and walked into the room.

The red haired female closed the doors behind us, but I didn't turn back to look. I already felt trapped enough as it was.

Ahead of me, a raised dias that probably usually held the throne, had six small chairs sitting on it. Two of the chairs were empty. My chest tightened as I recalled Jaya, the council member who had provided me with the second trial. She'd given me a correct trial and she'd ensured that I didn't return to the location I started from. I knew she'd probably saved my life.

I tore my eyes away from the empty chair and looked at the other members of the council. The red haired Fae settled herself into one of the empty chairs.

I waited patiently, unsure of how this was supposed to work. Were they waiting for me to address them? After a few awkward moments of silence, I lowered myself into a curtsy. "Council."

"Welcome, Cassia," the red haired woman said. "Do you know why we are here?"

"To address my third trial," I said.

"Correct," Red replied. "You are here because you are asking for special permission to be granted to you after you've already been extended special permission to compete in the first place."

My brow furrowed. "I'm sorry, I don't know what you mean."

She lifted a perfectly sculpted red eyebrow. "Oh? Did nobody tell you changelings were illegal?"

"Yes, I've heard that," I said.

"So you realize that you shouldn't even be here," Red said.

"I—" I didn't know how to respond to that. I knew changelings were illegal, but I never thought about potential consequences.

"We granted you permission to compete due to the fact that

you were a child and the decisions to hide you were not yours to make," Red said.

"That's true," I mumbled.

"However, the decision to skip the third trial was not out of your hands. You are capable of making your own decisions now, I gather?" she asked.

I weighed her words carefully, realizing that there was a risk of answering incorrectly. I decided no answer was best. "I was given a third trial envelope as delivered by someone I trusted who was actually Tiana in disguise. She lured me away and attempted to kill me."

"The rules are clear," a male Fae said. "There are no allowable excuses for missing a trial. Candidates who miss one are out of the running for Queen."

"Surly, there can be an exception to this since I thought I was given the third trial?" I asked.

"No exceptions," another male said. "That's the rules."

"Surly, this is an unusual situation," I said.

"Of course it is," Red said. "But you even being in the trials is unusual as well. Queens aren't even allowed to have children. We've already made enough exceptions for you."

"But that hasn't always been the rules," I said. "You used to allow changelings and Queens used to have children."

"Yes, they did," one of the males said. "And we all paid too high a price during those times. Don't think you're special because of who you are."

"You realize whoever wins this is going to come after me, don't you?" I asked.

"Do you even want to be Queen?" Red asked.

"Of course, I do," I said, surprising myself with how sure I sounded. Maybe everyone else's faith in me was finally rubbing off on me.

"What makes you different? If we did this, we'd be breaking the rules for you again," one of the males said.

"I never asked you to break the rules for me before," I said. "As you mentioned, that wasn't my doing. This wasn't my doing, either, yet you blame me. And that's fine. I should be more observant and I have learned my lesson. But I can tell you, I will be an amazing Queen. I'm honest and fair. I believe in good and peace. I want what is best for Faerie, even if I'm new to learning about everything, I'm all in. This is what I was born to do."

"Even if we made an exception," Red said. "There's still the issue of the incomplete trial."

"Let me do it now," I said. "Let me show you."

Bang. Bang. Bang.

The council stopped talking and they looked past me to whatever was causing the disruption. I turned just in time to see the doors to the throne room swing open.

Jaya strode into the room, her dress torn and bloody. She had a long cut on her cheek and smudges of dirt on her face. Her hair hung loose and wild around her face, but she held her chin high.

Next to her, looking equally worse for wear stood Tristan.

Chapter Twenty-Eight

M y heart leaped and I let out a choked cry as I our eyes met. He was here and he was alive.

Tristan's blond hair had been pulled back in a hasty tail giving me a clear view of his dirt covered face. A tear in the fabric on his shoulder revealed a wound that had sent crimson blood soaking into his tunic.

My forehead creased in concern. I wanted to run to him, but I knew I had to maintain my composure here. The council was about to eliminate my chance of becoming Queen and I couldn't show any signs of weakness.

Nani? I mouthed the word, hoping Tristan caught my question.

Safe, he mouthed back.

I let out a sigh of relief.

"What is the meaning of this?" Red asked.

I turned to see her descending the dias. "Jaya, what happened? We've been trying to reach you for days." She turned to Tristan. "Is this your doing? Have you followed in your father's footsteps?"

"Stop, Amala. The Winter Prince saved my life because she asked him to." Jaya lifted her chin toward me.

The red haired female, Amala, looked over at me. "Why was she in danger in the first place? What game are you playing with the Winter Prince?"

"No game," I said, feeling the truth of the words. Tristan's plans had always felt like games to me before. Like he was hiding thing from me for his own gain. Now, I knew his reasons weren't for his own interest. He was protecting his home and protecting me. "I was a guest at his palace, as you know since my first trial was sent there. Then, the Winter King kidnapped me."

"He intercepted me on my way to the Winter Palace," Jaya said. "I never reached Cassia. He held us both."

"How do you fit into all of this?" Amala asked Tristan.

"He's the new king," Jaya said.

My stomach twisted into knots and a chill ran down my spine. "You did it." The words came out so quiet, I wasn't even sure I'd said them.

Tristan gave me a quick half-smile before fixing a more serious expression on his face. "My father was a tyrant. He caused the war that split Faerie and he brought nothing but pain to anyone who ever crossed his path. He has been eliminated."

Amala's face twitched and she blinked a few times. Then, she inclined her head. "Congratulations on your victory, your highness."

Tristan nodded but didn't respond.

Jaya walked away from us, toward the empty chair.

"Jaya," Amala said, "I'm sure you're exhausted from your ordeal, shouldn't you rest?"

"A candidate cannot be removed from Queen's Trial unless the entire council votes on it. How were you planning to acquire my vote?" Jaya asked.

The timid female I'd seen held captive by the Winter King was gone, replaced by a warrior.

"We hadn't heard from you for days," Amala said, walking toward her seat. "We feared the worst."

"Yet, you still set up six chairs," she said.

"Forgive me, high priestess," Amala said, lowering herself into a curtsy at Jaya's feet.

"Have a seat, Amala. Let's finish this," Jaya said.

I couldn't help but smile as Amala quietly took her place, deferring her power to Jaya.

"You may take your leave, your highness," Amala said to Tristan.

"No," Jaya said. "He stays."

Amala shriveled a bit in her chair, her confidence visibly reduced.

I held my chin high, keeping my eyes on the Council. I couldn't see Tristan, but I could feel his presence. It comforted me and gave me the boost of strength I needed to finish this.

I curtsied to Jaya. "Priestess, it's good to see you again."

"You as well," Jaya said. "I'm glad you were smart enough to find your way out of the trial and back into safety."

Seeing her poise and leadership here, I realized her entire terrified persona might have been an act. If I made it through this, I wanted Jaya close. She was exactly the type of counsel that could aid a ruler in making clear decisions. "Thank you for your help."

"Thank you for asking your mate to help us," she said.

Mate. The word sounded so natural coming from Jaya. Nobody flinched. It made me wonder if I had been the last to know. Was the connection between the two of us so obvious that even strangers saw it?

"You showed great strength under pressure. You were able to keep your head and focus on the trial even with so much going on that was beyond your control," Jaya added.

I took a deep breath in and lowered my gaze, staring at my borrowed boots. I didn't feel brave at the time, I just did what I thought needed done. I looked back up at Jaya.

"Am I to understand that the candidate missed the final trial?" Jaya asked the others.

"She did, indeed," one of the males answered.

"And what did you create for the final trial in my absence?" she asked.

"Each candidate was given a puzzle box they had to open with magic." Amala glanced at me, then looked back at Jaya. "It's vital to have a firm grasp of how to use magic under pressure for a Queen."

"A puzzle box?" Jaya asked.

The members of the council fidgeted in their seats. A couple of them cleared their throats.

"We have a candidate who battled Tiana while facing a creature of the Under and you want to eliminate her because she didn't complete a puzzle box?" Jaya lifted an eyebrow.

None of the other council members spoke.

"I request a vote," Jaya said. "Those in favor of allowing the candidate to move on to the physical trials?"

Jaya extended her hand in the air. Two female Fae who hadn't spoken raised their hands. Then, slowly, the two male Fae raised their hand. Finally, Amala's hand stretched into the air.

Jaya lowered her hand and the others followed. "It's settled, then. Cassia, congratulations. You're moving on to the physical trials."

My shoulders dropped as the tension I held released. "Thank you."

Jaya smiled and inclined her head.

Amala glared at me. I turned away from her, knowing I'd have to keep her on my good side for the next part of this process.

The members of the council stood and walked away from their chairs. One by one, they filed out past me into the hall where I knew Ethan, Dane, and Cormac were eagerly waiting to hear what happened.

Tristan grabbed my hand as I watched the council members leave. "Are you alright?"

"Me?" I almost laughed. "You're the one who was in a battle." I reached for his injured shoulder.

He turned away from me. "It's nothing,"

"Don't do that to me," I said.

"Do what?" he asked.

"Shut me out," I said. "No more pretending. We need each other. You know that. I know that."

Out of the corner of my eye, I caught a glimpse of Ethan, Dane, and Cormac waiting in the hallway. They stood just outside the door, ready to run to me if I called to them.

"That might be true," he said. "But how are you going to explain that to the rest of them?"

"They're going to have to accept it," I said.

"That's not going to be as easy as you think," he said.

"Nothing worth doing is ever easy," I said. "You know that. Probably more than anyone."

"Cassia."

My knees wobbled at the sound of my name on his lips, coming out as if he were saying a prayer. "Yes?"

"If you want me, I'm yours," he said.

"I want you," I said.

"I was hoping you'd say that." He leaned down and pressed his lips to mine.

I kissed him back, knowing that I was going to have a lot of explaining to do once this kiss ended.

Author Notes

Thank you for taking the time to read my book! I hope you enjoyed your time with Cassia and her princes!

Be the first to hear when Book 4 is available!
Join My List

Also by Dyan Chick
Magic Born, Dragon Mage Book 1
Magic Awakens, Dragon Mage Book 2
Magic Rising, Dragon Mage Book 3
Magic Returns, Dragon Mage Book 4
Fae Cursed: Legacy of Magic Book 1
Dark Fae: Legacy of Magic Book 2
Heir of Illaria: Book 1 of the Illaria Series
Oracle of Illaria: Book 2 of the Illaria Series
Battle of Illaria: Book 3 of the Illaria Series